CALL
THE DARKNESS
DOWN

CALL THE DARKNESS DOWN

Dixie Tenny

A Margaret K. McElderry Book

Atheneum   1984   *New York*

"Pan Ddaw'r Dydd" is reprinted with the kind permission of
Geraint Jarman who wrote the lyrics.

Library of Congress Cataloging in Publication Data

Tenny, Dixie.
Call the darkness down.

"A Margaret K. McElderry book."
Summary: Morfa Owen, an American studying at a college in
Wales while searching for traces of her Welsh grandparents,
receives a series of mysterious messages before realizing that
someone or something is trying to kill her.
[1.   Wales—Fiction.   2.   Grandparents—Fiction.
3.   Mystery and detective stories]   I.   Title.
PZ7.T26398Ca   1984   [Fic]   83–15484
ISBN 0–689–50289–3

To my nephew,
Nathan Edward Tenny,
with thanks for your confidence,
your assistance
and your impatience

I would like to thank the following people for their help and/or encouragement: my parents, Dai Parker-Gwilliam, Pam Parker, Ora Hayes, Nancy Hammond, Louise Smith, Kennett Lehmann, Mike Bruss, Lucille Fischer, Gwen Wellington, Sherri Lux, and the members of Fools Face, with special gratitude to Eleanor Cameron and Mr. Bass for taking me on my first trip to Wales many years ago.

"The old church tower and garden wall
Are black with autumn rain,
And dreary winds foreboding call
The darkness down again."

Emily Jane Brontë
October, 1837

Contents

CALL
THE DARKNESS
DOWN

1

Going Away

"Well, I think you're a perfect idiot," Sheena said.

My cousin glared at me from under the window, where she sat curled with Lara the Airedale's head pillowed on her lap. The breeze from the revolving fan on my desk swirled her hair around briefly, then mine. It was a relief; my room was sultry from the late Missouri summer beating in fiercely through the windows. My brother Ethan lay stretched out on my bed, ruffling the ears of the tiny Airedale pup on his stomach. When Sheena spoke he turned his head and watched me with interest.

"It isn't that I don't want to go," I protested feebly. "It's just that I'm not sure about it." I shifted uneasily in the big rocker. "I mean, maybe I'd be happier staying here and going to Missouri University like you, Ethan. A lot of my friends are going there. Or maybe I should stay in Kansas City and work in the secretarial pool with you, Sheen . . ."

"Listen, cuz." Sheena tapped Lara on the head for emphasis. "You're cute, but you're not very bright. Oh all right, you're bright enough sometimes. Not about this. Do you think I'm staying here and working in the stupid secretarial pool because that's what I want to do? Where was I when you were taking the qualifying tests for foreign study? Right there taking them too, wasn't I? The only difference is that you made the grade and I didn't. Or I'd be packing my bags right now: correct?"

This was true. I was sorry I had brought the subject up at all. I had forgotten how much Sheena had wanted to go to Wales. "I'm sorry. It must seem horribly ungrateful of me to talk like this, when I was the lucky one."

"Apology unnecessary but accepted." She wiped a bead of sweat from her forehead and smiled at me. "Listen. I know we got interested in Wales in the beginning because our mothers were born there. But your attitude has never been like theirs about it, you know. Take the language, for instance. Mum and Aunt Gwenfair were born in Wales and grew up there but never learned to speak the language, like at least half of their generation. That doesn't bother them at all, but you think it's terrible. I guess Ethan and I do too"—Ethan nodded, staring at the ceiling—"but not as much as you, because languages and their relation to a country's history have always been your speacial 'thing.' As long as I can remember, not counting silly kid things, you've wanted to be a—a—"

"—research historian—"

"—a research historian, and help people understand themselves better through gaining knowledge of their languages and their histories, right?"

"Right, but—"

"Well, isn't that something you want to find out about during your year in Wales? It's an English-speaking country with a language of its own that is dying, and you want to see if people care, and if they're trying to revive it, don't you? Our mothers couldn't care less about something like that. If you think hard, I imagine you'll find that the Wales you want to see for yourself is a different one from the one our mothers love and grew up in. That's why I wanted to go there; not to live the way our mothers lived when they were young, but to learn the language and read about Welsh history the way the Welsh saw it, not the English who conquered them. And to find out if there are people living there, Welsh people, to whom history and myths and language mean something more than they did to our mothers."

I stopped rocking and stared at the silver-green Russian olive leaves outside my window. Sheena was right. As much as Mam loved Wales, she considered herself "British," not "Welsh," which had always upset me. How could you lump together such different people, with such different pasts, as the Welsh, the English, the Scots and the Irish, and call them all by the same name? Especially because I had read enough Welsh literature to know that there was still deeply rooted hostility between the Welsh and the English, due to the way the Welsh had been oppressed when the English had first conquered Wales. And I was loyal to Wales, of course . . . because of my mother.

Gwenfair Morgan, now Gwenfair Owen, had grown up in the lush green hills of South Wales. Through her, my brothers, my sister and I grew up there too. When she told us stories of her youth, we went to open-air markets on Saturday mornings, played around standing stones in vast, wheat-colored fields, explored caves in the hills, never drifted far from the sound and scent of the sea. Her yearning for her home country had become our yearning, without, I now realized, our ever really deciding that going there was something we wanted to do for ourselves. It wasn't that Mam had encouraged me to apply for the foreign study program and take the tests; she had seemed, instead, perversely reluctant about it. But she had already poured so much of her love for Wales into me that I looked forward to my trip as if I were the one going home. That is, until I found myself two days away from my date with the airplane. Now, suddenly and belatedly, I began to wonder if I, Morfa Owen, really wanted to go. After all, if things got difficult, there could be no comforting phone calls to Sheena, Ethan or Sam. I would travel alone, arrive alone, and if I didn't get along with my Welsh college-mates, remain for a year inescapably alone.

"Hey." Ethan poked me in the knee with an argyled foot. "It's natural to have butterflies, kid. I had them when I left for M.U. the first time. I didn't know anyone there either, you know, but of course I made friends right away. You will too."

"But Ethan, what if I don't? It's one thing to go a hundred miles away to a college where everyone was brought up pretty much as you were, but Wales? What if we don't understand each other and don't get along? They speak English in Wales, but you and I know that deep down they aren't the same as we are at all."

Ethan shook his head. "You're forgetting a couple of pretty important things, Morfa. First, you and I were raised by a Welshwoman. Half, at *least* half of what we think and how we feel was molded by someone who was brought up in that culture. Of course, after you started to school you had a lot of other influences, but what you experience first is what sticks with you. I'm sure you'll do fine."

"And you're going to Wales through a special program," Sheena said. "They send Americans over every year, don't they?"

"Yes, about thirty to different universities and colleges."

"Well? You won't be alone with your difficulties, then, whatever they may be. There will be other Americans—"

"But I don't want to go all the way to Wales to meet other Americans! I'm going there to meet Welsh people—"

"I know! But they *will* be there, and they will be what

you're used to. Just because you don't want to spend your day in the pool at the shallow end, that doesn't mean you can't head back there every now and then for a few minutes when you begin to lose your breath in the deep end.

"But you jumped the gun anyway. I wasn't going to suggest hanging out with other Americans. I was just going to point out that you will probably be the one of them best prepared to cope with whatever you find over there. Because you've been raised on our mothers' stories, *you,* at least, know how to pronounce weird Welsh names like Aberystwyth and Llanelli. And you know enough not to offend the natives by calling them English or something like that. I bet you'll be the only one who'll know those things. Or one of just a few, anyway. You'll probably come off looking cool and organized while the others spend their first days in Wales totally embarrassed."

I thought this over for a long time. Ethan set Freya, the puppy, down by Lara and began to flip idly through one of my books. Sheena unbuttoned another button on her shirt and watched me patiently.

Finally I said "They may not want to make friends with Americans at all, you know. I'm Welsh over here, but over there I'll just be American."

Ethan closed the book with a snap. "You're absolutely right, kiddo. They may not want to. I haven't the slightest idea how they feel about Americans. But Morfa, if they do turn out to be a bunch of bigoted Nationalists, there's nothing that you can do about it. I doubt that they are— this program you're going on has been sending thirty Americans to Wales each year for a long time, and I doubt enrollment would keep up like that if the ones who went came back with reports of hostile natives. Don't you think? But if that's how it is, just plunge into your books and the scenery, and get to know the other Americans. And if you do have some extra time on your hands, maybe you can visit Trevaughan."

Somehow I had expected this. And below the language, the history, the literature and the experience, this lay at the heart of my reason for wanting to go to Wales.

Mam had told me stories about her home country all of my life. I probably got rocked to sleep as a baby by "Cwm Rhondda" instead of "Brahms' Lullaby." She talked about every tiny detail of her life in Wales—except why she left. Whenever the subject of Mam's parents came up, the conversation was cut short. Sheena had the same experience with her mother, my Aunt Angharad, Mam's twin sister. Finally Dad took Ethan, Sheena and me aside one day and told us that Mam's parents were the one subject he had never been able to get her to talk about, even with him. That she had suggested some still-painful memory of a tragedy connected with them and asked that they never be mentioned again. So there was no pressing the issue, but we wondered often what had happened to our Morgan grandparents.

My high school counsellor had shown me several college programs in Wales. Instead of a program at a large university, I had chosen one at a small college in a town called Carmarthen . . . because Carmarthen was very close to Trevaughan, where my mother had grown up.

I looked from Ethan to Sheena. "You think I might be able to find out what happened to Gran and Grandad Morgan."

They nodded. Sheena said quietly, "It seems important, somehow, to know who your grandparents were, and what they were like. You might even meet people over there who knew them."

I turned to Ethan. "Do you know anything at all about

our Morgan grandparents? Surely 'Morgan' is an incredibly common Welsh name. We know that Mam and Aunt Angharad came to the United States about twenty-five years ago, but I don't know anything else at all. Do you?"

Ethan frowned. "I may be the oldest and the smartest— don't argue, junior—but age seems to have no privilege where this is concerned. Mam hasn't said a thing to me. It's so frustrating! All we've ever heard all our lives is Wales this and Wales that, Wales the Promised Land, the Island Paradise. Well, if Wales is so all-fired perfect, why did they leave? All alone, just the two of them barely out of their teens, knowing nobody over here at all. Even if there was a tragedy, surely they would have wanted to be with their friends, or at least in their country! It seems as if there must have been more to it than that."

"A mystery, or a scandal, you mean?" Sheena shrugged. "I always just assumed that the association with the parents' death was too painful for them to stay."

"If your parents suddenly died, would you pack up and leave the country?"

Sheena looked at the top of Lara's head. I said, "It does seem pretty strange, doesn't it? They talk about everything up to their leaving school and then, 'cut'. As if they took off their caps and gowns, stuck their diplomas in their back pockets and hopped on the boat for America. Why won't they at least talk about their last years there? I don't understand it at all."

We all fell silent. The heat was stifling, and suddenly I felt the need for something cold to drink.

I stood up and said, "I'm going to the kitchen. Coming?"

Sheena pushed Lara's head off her lap and got up. Ethan swung around and sat up, then poked me in the elbow.

"You have to go, you know. Sheena and I can't, at least not yet, and this is important."

I grabbed his hand and pulled him to his feet. "Yes, I'll go. I want to know as badly as you do. But don't expect too much. A common last name, a vague hint of a tragedy and an approximate year of when Mam left Wales isn't much to go on."

"I know," said Ethan, patting me on the back.

There was a great deal of noise at my going-away party the next day.

If this had been another short trip, even three months like last summer, it would have been different. But a year is a long time, so everyone had to be invited, from my smallest second cousin to the neighbor at the farthest end of the street. And if some of them hadn't seen me since junior high school, they hadn't seen each other in as long either. Children had to be compared, illnesses discussed, politics argued over genially. Little knots all over the field behind our house became bigger knots, and mumble grew to buzz to hum. I heard Mam thank "the Powers That Be" half a dozen times that day that it hadn't rained.

Grandpa Owen, who was hard of hearing, hugged me when he arrived and immediately fell asleep in the living room. The twins—Mam and Aunt Angharad—fixed lemonade for everyone, while Dad, Uncle Ted, a variety of cousins and the members of my younger brother Sam's band played baseball in the field. Older relatives and neighbors sat in a ring of lawn chairs around the wide, open porch, chatting and watching the baseball game. Sheena played badminton with Bird, my across-the-street neighbor, while my little sister Meg entertained Bird's toddler son. Pausing in my rounds to watch Bird and Sheena, I had a fleeting, sinking feeling that they were already closing ranks, already adjusting, and all too easily, to my being gone.

Finally Mam whistled us all in to the porch, where drinks and a chocolate-chip angel food cake had been set on the table by her and Aunt Angharad. There was a brief confusion of hand-washing and child-counting. Then everyone gathered around the table and raised their drinks in a good luck toast to my trip.

This was the family's Cake Ceremony. Every time a party was held for a member of our family, the guest of honor cut her own cake. As she handed each piece to a relative or friend, he named one good thing that he hoped would happen to her during the coming year. This time, the wishes were for my trip.

I handed the first piece to Mam. Looking at her, still very pretty, with dark, thick hair and hazel eyes like my own, I thought suddenly of her together in the kitchen all morning with her sister preparing this. I wondered if, when the two of them were alone, they spoke of the things they would never discuss with their families.

Mam smiled, took the cake and said, "I hope you get to spend some time at Llansteffan Castle." She sighed. "It was my favorite spot in all of South Wales."

The next piece went to Aunt Angharad, who said, "I hope you get to see an International Rugby game, Morfa! They're wonderful. Everyone sings to encourage the team, and—"

"Angharad, dear, the children are starving!" said Uncle Ted.

Everyone laughed, Aunt Angharad with them. "Well, then, there we are. You've heard it a dozen times anyway."

"Thanks, Aunt Angharad. Sheena?"

Sheena leaned forward with wicked eyes and winked. "I hope you meet a handsome Welshman," she whispered loudly, and I punched her in the arm as everyone laughed again and applauded.

"I hope you stay healthy."

"I hope you don't get run over by a double-decker bus!"

"I hope you aren't lost the whole time on the London Underground."

"I hope you come back piled down with presents."

"I hope you meet a *rich* Welshman."

"I hope you don't get thrown in jail or deported."

"I hope you find some old lost treasure," said Ethan, and I looked at him, and then at Sheena.

"I hope so, too," I said.

There was a wait at Kansas City International Airport after I checked my bags. Mam, Dad, Ethan and I made small talk for a while. Then Ethan suggested he and I go buy soft drinks for all of us. When we were out of sight of Mam and Dad, he stopped me.

"I know something that might help you find our grandparents," he said quietly. He pushed me through the milling crowd to a niche by the phone booths, where we could talk undisturbed.

"Ethan, what is it?"

Ethan stared at me for a moment, then said "You know that when I was in high school, Mam and Dad sold me their old Plymouth to use getting to and from work."

I nodded.

"Well, on the day that I was going to take the registration to City Hall to get it changed into my name, I went to Mam and asked for the key to the strongbox, where the registration was kept. She was absorbed in something at the time, and handed me her ring of keys without paying much attention. So I went downstairs and opened the box, and the first document that I found was Mam's birth certificate. Just as I unfolded it, I heard her running down the stairs, calling that she would get the registration for me because there were some private papers in the box. So I folded it up quickly and shoved it back in. She never knew that I saw it at all. Not that I saw much. But I did see her father's first name, and I remember it because luckily for me, it was short and odd."

"What was it?"

"Y-n-y-r. How's that for a name? I have no idea how to pronounce it and I'm not going to try. And it may be as common as John over there. But it's a clue, anyway. Anything you can find on Y-n-y-r Morgan of Trevaughan, South Wales, who died tragically some twenty-odd years ago."

"Y-n-y-r Morgan," I repeated, testing the name and memorizing it.

"Morfa? Ethan?"

I jumped as Dad spoke right behind me.

"What are you two talking so seriously about? Didn't you hear your flight called, Morfa?"

"No! When?"

"A few minutes ago, You'd better hurry, now. You can get something to drink on the plane."

He put one arm around my shoulders and one around Ethan's as we headed back toward my gate. Ethan and I looked at each other, wishing we had a chance to discuss Mam's birth certificate, but that chance never came.

Fifteen minutes later the plane was off the ground, circling over Kansas City and then heading northeast toward the ancient land that kept my mother's secret.

2

Carmarthen

The lamp across the room created enough light to make writing possible—barely. I sat at my plain wooden desk by the window, two flights up, that overlooked a lane running through Carmarthen College grounds. The lane was just wide enough for one car. Trees grew here and there along it, and beyond them Dewi Hostel loomed vaguely. To the left, the lane curved around the chapel and the Academic Building and behind them, down a small wooded hill to the canteen, out of sight. There were fields to the far right beyond the big stone entry gates, then hills on hills and, tonight, stars on stars. I had never dreamed of being able to see so many stars, sweeping in a patterned, shadowed spiral across the wide, cool sky.

I had cranked the window open and a light breeze drifted across the desk. Though I shivered a bit, the air smelled too clean and fresh to shut out. I leaned forward for one long, last look at the empty lane, then chose a pen from the cupful on the desk and folded my notebook back to a blank page.

2B. Mair Hostel
Coleg Caerfyrddin
Caerfyrddin, Dyfed
Cymru
September 14.

Dear Ethan,

Yes, here I am in Wales—or Cymru, as they say it in Welsh—at last! It's pronounced KUM-ree, by the way. Like my address? "Mair" is the Welsh version of "Mary," after St. Mary, and they say "hostel" instead of "dormitory." The second line is the name of the college, and it translates "Carmarthen College." It's pronounced "KO-leg kire-VUR-thun." Dyfed (DUH-ved) is the county Carmarthen is in. As you can tell, I've actually picked up a little Welsh already! But those are all names that you hear over and over again around here. I'm not quite fluent yet! But first things first: my trip here.

It was a LONG plane ride, but not bad at all, because I slept almost all the way! I missed both dinner and the movie, and when I woke up and looked out the window, Ireland was stretched out all beautiful and green below! I could hardly believe it. The flight ended about half an hour after that at Gatwick Airport. What a place! A million people, coming and going at top speed in all directions. The customs man asked a lot of questions—I think he guessed the truth, that I am actually a top international spy—but the certification papers the college had sent me fooled him and he let me into the country. I gathered up my luggage and caught a train to Victoria Station, like the instructions said. That's when I really started to feel as if I were thousands of miles away from everyone, and instead of being afraid the way I thought I would be, I felt terribly grownup and self-sufficient. It was wonderful! I took the Underground from Victoria to

Paddington Station. That was amazing! I felt like someone in an old black-and-white British spy thriller. All those men swinging on and straight into a seat, and I swear they hadn't been sitting for two seconds before their newspapers snapped open and they were reading, nonchalant as you please! I can't imagine how they knew when they had reached their stations, because they never looked up until the subway would stop and suddenly the paper was folded up and they went swinging off! All those brown and gray tweeds . . . And the insides of the subway trains were plastered with advertising posters for everything you could imagine. Anyway, I had a sandwich at Paddington while I was waiting for the 1:35 to Swansea—fortunately I had remembered to change my money at the airport! The coins and bills here are big! The ride to Swansea was a couple of hours long, and at the end of the line in Swansea I switched trains for the last time, destination Carmarthen!

The scenery here is so beautiful, it's hard to believe without seeing it. Lush, green farmland, all divided into little squares by tall hedges or squat stone walls. No barbed wire, hurray! And the farms roll up and down with the hills. They seem like a part of the natural scenery, instead of like they're fighting against it. A big river sparkled alongside the tracks. I found out later that it's the River Towy, and it flows through downtown Carmarthen. Once, when we rounded a sudden curve, there across the river on a high bluff rose a great gray castle ruin! Then the bluffs opened up and there was a glimpse of the sea.

A minibus from the college was at the Carmarthen station to meet me and the two other Americans who were on the train. We said hello to each other, but not much else because the bus lurched off right away and we were all anxious to see what Carmarthen was going to be like. Our "hometown" for the next year.

I could hardly believe it, Ethan. It was a giant step out of the twentieth century . . . The streets are steep, narrow and cobbled; they look as if goat carts and horses should be traveling on them, not cars! Our Thunderbird would NOT fit. No neon signs, no stoplights, no huge department stores, no smoke belching from factories. The streets wander casually between tall rows of old-fashioned shops and houses attached side-to-side with each other. They reminded me a little of houses I saw last summer in San Francisco. Small cars darted here and there; the intersections have what is called "roundabouts" instead of traffic signs or lights. This means that the cars, instead of stopping to wait for each other, all whisk into a little circle, zoom around it all at once, and exit through the opening that goes in whatever direction they're headed. A great system, I think! We passed an ancient-looking tiny church tucked within a neat circular graveyard; then across the street I saw an old castle wall jutting up behind a row of shops.

And the *people*, Ethan! Lines of them wound up and down the streets on impossibly narrow sidewalks and in and out of the shops . . . ladies pushing baby buggies, men with round, wrinkled faces and sporting flat tweed caps, knots of women on corners with baskets over their arms talking and gesturing at a great rate, a bunch of schoolchildren in uniforms dashing out the front door of a tall brick school . . . well, so much for my fears that Carmarthen might be modernized and tasteless! It's hard to believe, but it seems that the old, graceful Wales that you and I were told stories about still exists.

The bus creaked up a road that led away from the town; I saw a sign that read "Ffordd Glannant/Glannant Road." Tall stone walls rose on both sides of the bus and when we met a car coming (*quickly*) toward us, I knew we were going to scrape. But we didn't. Then the walls gave way to a double row of lovely private homes with front yards; the words "miniature Roman villas" came to mind. They probably look like nothing of the sort. A sweep of empty field, a series of pastures complete with grazing cows, and we were turning in through the curved stone gates that are the entrance to Carmarthen College.

I set my pen down and flexed my fingers, then swiveled this way and that in the chair until my back popped satisfyingly. I listened for a few moments, but there was no sound from out in the hall. I decided to rush through the rest of Ethan's letter, before writer's cramp set in all over my body!

We were met by the Director of American Studies, a short, curly-haired, person named Robert Engels. ("Call me Rob.") His job is to arrange our field trips, help us make out our class schedules, introduce us to the ten or twelve Welsh students who came to college early to help us get oriented. (Classes don't begin until next week, when the rest of the students will arrive.) And he listens to our gripes, etc. He seems nice enough. A young, enthusiastic guy with a bit of Boston or someplace near in his accent. As soon as we dropped our luggage off in our rooms, he gave us a guided tour of the campus.

There are five hundred students here, Ethan, and I remember your saying Missouri U has about 23,000!

There are four hostels in which we all live—no private apartments allowed, even if there are any close by, which I doubt. My hostel (Mair) and the one for boys across the lane (Dewi—Welsh for "David" and also named after a saint) are yellow brick and appear to be about a hundred years old. The other two are down the lane near the canteen, or cafeteria. They're pretty buildings, and the lane is lined with trees and lots of rose bushes. The red roses, which are still blooming here, smell like cinnamon!

There's only one building on campus where classes are held, and it's called the Academic Building, originally enough! There is an infinitely tiny library in it. Two more buildings in all—one is the canteen, and the other is the Student Union. The Union has a wide dance floor and stage, lots of comfortable chairs, an enclosed upper floor with a TV room, pinball machines, a little store—which carries necessities like biscuits and college sweat shirts, a Ping-Pong table, dartboards, a pool table, a jukebox and a bar! Tremendous . . .

The campus is surrounded by woods and fields, and the famous Welsh hills stretch away in all directions. I can hardly wait to get out and start exploring them!

The pen clattered back into its cup, and I snapped my notebook shut. There was more to tell but it would have to wait. I leaned back on the legs of my chair and looked over my room. A dividing wall that also served as a bookcase hid my roommate's bed and one washbasin. The walls were bare and white now, but soon they would be covered with posters, the shelves with books and mementoes of hikes and shopping trips, the big bulletin board with pictures of new places and new acquaintances—or at least my share of them. I was looking forward to it, but I was also enjoying the looking-forward itself, with my entire experience in Wales still to come. It was exciting; a whole year of new adventures was on the brink of beginning . . .

I jumped at a loud rap on the door, then called, "Coming!"

I opened the door and there stood a blonde elf.

Well, not an elf really, but a slender, small, blonde girl with a pointed nose and pixieish eyes, who looked as if she certainly had elf ancestors. However, her accent when she spoke was as American as my own.

"Hi! I'm Laney West; Elaine, really, but don't mind that. I saw the light under your door and thought I'd stop by and talk for a minute or two if you aren't busy . . ."

"Not at all!" She beamed and we shook hands. I waved her into the room and shut the door behind her. "My name's Morfa Owen."

"What an unusual name!"

"It's Welsh. It's spelled M-o-r-f-a, but the 'f' is pronounced 'v.' Have a seat."

"Thanks." Laney sat on the bed, wriggling into the lotus position. I returned to my desk chair and put my feet up on the windowsill.

"How did you come by a Welsh name?"

"My mother is Welsh. She and my aunt were brought up in Trevaughan, a little town just a hill or two over from here."

"Aha." Laney squinted at me, then said, "But you speak like an American."

I laughed. "I *am* an American! Born and brought up in Kansas City, Missouri. My mam left Wales long before I was born. Where are you from?"

"San Francisco, California."

"Mmm . . . that's a beautiful city. I was out there with some of my cousins last summer, and I could hardly bear to leave. What brings you to Wales?"

"Boredom," Laney answered promptly, then grinned. "I have a lot of friends at home who are pretty well off, and after we graduated from high school last spring a bunch of them took off to "do Europe" for a year. Some to go to college there and some just to travel around, you know, to recover from the terrible strain of studying and taking finals, poor things! Well, I am *not* well off, but I had worked part-time during school and full-time summers, so I had some money in the bank. So I decided all of a sudden that I would go to Europe, too! A fun way to start college. But when my friends started asking whether I was going to Paris or Stockholm, or *poss*-ibly London, though that's a bit low-brow, *dah*-ling"—I laughed at Laney's affected accent—"I decided to go to the tiniest, most obscure college in the smallest, least-fashionable country I could find. So, while Estelle Bingham-Jones suns her delicate body in the heart of fleur-de-lis country, Laney West will be tramping through muddy cow pastures in the land of the leek."

Laney wrinkled her nose, looking so perplexed at herself that I burst out laughing, and she broke down and laughed too. We talked for a long time, about our friends, about school, and about our families.

"So even though your mother grew up in Wales, you've never been here before?"

"Right." Uncomfortable suddenly, I added, "We're such a big family, it would have cost a fortune to fly us all over."

"Don't think I don't envy you that big family! Being one of six might not be great all of the time, but let me assure you that being one of one is the last word in boring. But what about your Welsh grandparents? You mean your mother hasn't seen them in—how old did you say your brother is?—twenty-one years?"

"Ethan is twenty-one, but Mam and Aunt Angharad left Wales about twenty-five years ago. No, she hasn't seen them—hasn't been back here since then."

"Then they don't come and visit you either?"

"No, they never have . . ."

"For crying out loud! Do they send pictures in their letters? Do you even know what they look like?"

I hesitated. I had never spoken about my grandparents to anyone outside the family before, but I had a terrible urge to tell Laney about them. I wasn't sure at all why, because I had only known her for about an hour! There was just something about the frank, self-possessed San Franciscan who was *"not* well off" (I had my own suspicions about the truth of that) that made me want to confide in her. Why not, I decided. What could it hurt?

"Laney, I don't even know if they are alive."

She stared. "You're kidding! Aren't you?"

I shook my head. "I don't know if they were alive when Mam and Aunt Angharad left Wales twenty-five years ago. As far as we kids know, there's been absolutely no contact between them all that time, and Mam has never mentioned them. The few times we've dared to bring them up ourselves, we've been shut up pretty quickly. I don't know anything about them except that they lived in Trevaughan . . ." I shrugged.

"Wow." Laney's eyes shone greenly luminescent in the lamplight. "That is too weird. Is your mom usually the mysterious type?"

I laughed. "Not at all. She's a very down-to-earth person, very frank, and my aunt is the same. That's why this stands out so much. My cousin Sheena Davis has asked me to try to find out what I can about all this while I'm here. And

Ethan did the same thing. You see, they're both much more in tune with things that are mysterious than I am. I'm pretty much like my mam and my aunt. Down-to-earth, I mean. I've read King Arthur and Tolkien and the Ring cycle and the Mabinogion, but they've sort of faded out of my life now and real, everyday things have taken over. That didn't happen with Ethan and Sheena. The mystery and fantasy is still part of their "real worlds." The idea of mysteries and questing for missing persons seems perfectly run-of-the-mill to them, but deep down I'm almost sure that there will be some perfectly simple, probably dull explanation for all of this."

"What's the Mabinogion?"

"What? Oh. The Mab-in-O-ghe-un," I answered, gently correcting Laney's pronunciation, "is a cycle of Welsh hero tales along the general lines of Arthur and the Grail Quest. But much older, I think, and more outlandish. Severed heads bounding around and chattering away, and lots of dealings with the Underworld and so on. A lot of people die in gory ways, I remember."

"It sounds delightful."

"Actually, I remember loving it when I was younger. Isn't that disgusting? I don't know why. Maybe we'll study it here, since it's the big Welsh classic. Are you taking literature classes?"

"Well, I'm not sure yet. We'll be talking about schedules with Rob in the morning. Have you thought about asking if we could take harp lessons?"

Taken aback, I laughed and said, "Sure, it's been preying on my mind all summer long!"

Laney laughed, too, and reached across the bed to hit me. "I'm serious! Wouldn't it be the Welshest of Welsh things to do?"

Finally Laney stood and stretched. "Eeee-yow, that feels

good." She turned and fluffed the pillow she had been leaning against. "How long have we been talking? Is it time for breakfast yet?"

"Not quite." I looked at my watch. "It's a little after midnight, so you've been here for about two hours."

"Is that all? I'd better get upstairs to bed. I'm in room Ten B, top flight, this hall. Come up soon and often! It's really been fun . . . I was afraid that I'd get here and never meet anyone I liked the whole year long!"

"Me, too," I said wholeheartedly. "I'll come up and get you for breakfast—all right?"

"Great, as long as you promise not to show up before nine!"

"I promise." I got up and walked with Laney to the door. She stepped into the hall, then turned suddenly and said, "Don't think I've forgotten about your weird Welsh grandparents. Do you know anything else at all about them? Any clues? Any little bit of information that might help?"

I shook my head and said, "I've already told you that they lived in Trevaughan and that it was about twenty-five years ago that my mam left Wales. The only other thing I know is my grandfather's first name. At least I know how to spell it, but not how to say it yet. It's Y-n-y-r, and their last name was Morgan."

"Hm." Laney nodded solemnly. "That sure isn't much. But it's better than nothing. Good night!"

"Good night. I'll see you in the morning."

"Right!" And Laney raced up the stairs.

I reached for my pen. One last bit, and then this letter was going to be mailed, complete or not.

I've been gone about three hours now. Did you miss me? Bet you didn't even know I had left. But a blonde American elf came a knocking at my door . . . Her name is Laney West, and she's not exactly pretty but she's *cute*. You'd fall in love with her instantly. She's from San Francisco and seems to be a good person. We talked and talked, and somehow I ended up telling her about wanting to try and find out what happened to Gran and Grandad Morgan. She's very interested and I think she's planning to help. I can probably use all the help I can get, don't you think? I feel a little guilty about telling her, but that's stupid. Isn't it? It's nice to have made a friend already.

Two big hurdles to jump tomorrow. First, my scheduling of classes in the afternoon with Rob Engels. Then some of the Welsh students should be arriving—the ones who will be helping us orient ourselves. That shouldn't be threatening or frightening now, should it? But one of them, according to Rob, is my future roommate. I'm anxious to meet her—and I'm shaking in my boots.

Take good care of yourself, you big blond squirrel. Tell everyone hello for me, and write soon.

Love,
Morfa.

P.S. In the tell-me-another-tall-one department: Guess what Laney has talked me into doing. Taking harp lessons! Now that's something I'll use all my life! Do you think Sam's band could use a harpist? Maybe an electric harpist?

Love again,
M.

3 🦎

Friends

"It's Morfa, isn't it? Come on in, please; sit down."

Rob Engels rose briefly to shake my hand, then sat down again and pushed through the piles of papers on his heavily cluttered desk. I looked around for a place to sit, finally doubling up some stacks of books and perching uneasily on the edge of a rickety, black leather chair. Through the window behind Rob's desk, the tall, thin spire of the college chapel rose to split a smooth green hill behind it neatly in half.

"Aha." Rob brandished a folder triumphantly, then laid it on the desk and opened it. "Hm. So. This is your freshman year, is it? No previous college courses? Junior college? Night school?"

"No, nothing."

"Well, your high school grades are excellent. I'm sure you've heard all the usual horror stories about the British educational system. But Carmarthen College isn't Oxford, or Eton, or Rugby . . . have you read *Tom Brown's Schooldays?*"

"No." Thinking I had a vague grasp on what he was hinting at, I said, "How about *Jane Eyre?*"

Rob threw his head back and laughed a long, silent laugh. "It isn't Lowood, either! It's a good school, not as easy as American state universities but not at all impossible for a decent student. You should be able to keep up with your studies and have a full social schedule too. Met anyone yet?"

"Yes, Elaine West. And I had breakfast this morning with some of the other Americans . . . Lisa Braddock, and Karen and Jim Somebody-or-Other."

"Karen Collier, and Jim . . . there are two Jims. Tall and blond?"

"No, tall and dark."

"McNae. Tall, blond Jim is Larrison. Elaine West . . . her appointment was an hour or so ago. She mentioned wanting to look into harp lessons. Are you interested in that, too? It seems to me that your name came up."

"Yes, I'm interested. I have no experience with the harp, but I'd love to learn."

"Any musical experience at all?"

"Piano and saxophone."

"The saxophone won't do you much good, but the piano will help a lot. Now, about your other classes—have you looked over the course description booklet I sent you in the States?"

"Yes," and I dug into my jacket pocket. "Here. These are the ones I'd be most interested in taking. You didn't have meeting times in the booklet, so I don't know if any of them will conflict with each other or not."

"Let's see . . ." Rob began looking from my paper to the blocked-off schedule taped to the wall in front of his desk. "Yes, I think this should all fit together very nicely." He tore a sheet from a memo pad and began writing. "Welsh for Beginners from nine to eleven on Monday, Wednesday and Friday mornings. So you want to tackle the language, do you?"

"Yes." A little apprehension began to tingle up my spine, as Rob turned to frown at me.

"Isn't your mother Welsh?"

"That's right. She and my aunt grew up in Trevaughan."

"But not Welsh-speaking?"

"No."

"That's odd! Many of the Welsh south of here don't speak the language, but nearly all of your mother's generation as close as Trevaughan do. Well, there we are. I imagine there are plenty of exceptions. Only about twenty percent of the Welsh speak their own native language, you know."

"But *why?*"

Rob sighed and smiled at me, but I was deadly serious. "You're signed up for two history classes here. They'll do a much better job of explaining it to you than I can. It's all very long and complicated . . . but suffice it for the moment to say that at the time England conquered Wales, it didn't serve the purpose of the conquerors to have the conquered people able to plot rebellion right in front of their faces, in a language that they couldn't understand." And before I could complain that that certainly didn't apply to the present, since Wales had been conquered hundreds of years ago, Rob hurried on. "Now harp lessons, providing I can dig up a tutor, will be Monday, Wednesday and Friday afternoons from one to two o'clock, and your last class on those three days will be the History of Carmarthen and the Surrounding Communities, from four to six."

He consulted the sheet of paper and the schedule again and nodded. "Okay, then on Tuesdays and Thursdays, you'll have Creative Writing from ten to eleven. That's a tutorial, one-on-one. Do you write prose or poetry?"

"Oh, prose."

"Good. We have enough aspiring poets already. Your last class, History of the Celts, will be from two to four. That's three, six, nine, fourteen, sixteen credit hours in all. Does that suit you all right? I think it looks great."

"Sure—thanks."

"Here, then," and he handed me my paper back, with times and days of class meetings scribbled on it in pencil. "Congratulations! You are now a full-fledged Carmarthen College student." He glanced at the clock on his desk. "And in ten minutes, I get to do this all over again. Is there anything you want to ask me about? You've gotten the sheet that tells you about hostel rules and procedures?"

"Yes, it was on the desk in my room."

"Right. There aren't really many rules here; you'll find it strikingly different from high school! Just be sensible. You look like the sensible type. Don't skip classes unless you absolutely have to; that's one thing the lecturers don't like at all. Do try and study occasionally! They're pretty easy on the Americans here, because most of you have never been to Wales before and they know you want to spend a lot of time sightseeing. Have you gotten an orientation schedule yet?"

"No, I haven't."

"Can't get along without one of those!" Rob rummaged around through the piles on his desk and pulled out a sheet of slightly crumpled paper. He smoothed it and thrust it at me. "Here. Look this over and tell me if anything needs clarifying."

I began to read through each day's activities during orientation week, beginning that night. I don't know what I expected—seminars, maybe; meetings with professors, placement tests, but whatever it was, I was wrong! Walking tours, bus tours, folk nights, market visits, and mostly, night after night on the list, visits to the town pubs with Welsh students! My amazement must have been written all over my face, because Rob laughed.

"Well? Look. You don't need academic orientation. What can we possibly do for you in advance? You go to class, you take notes, you read the books, take finals and pass; or you skip class, don't take notes, don't read the books and fail. It's as simple as that. If you start classes and then find you have a problem, that's the time to come to me with it. But most of you won't—so, instead, we concentrate on what you're really going to need the most anyway—cultural orientation. It's not in the classroom that you're going to begin to feel lost and lonely. It's when class is out for the day and the long night stretches ahead of you . . . or when you need to go to town to buy shampoo and suddenly you realize that the people crammed all around you are speaking a language you don't understand, and the street names don't make sense either, and the cars buzzing past you are on the wrong side of the street."

I smiled back at him. "That makes a lot of sense. I really don't think I have any questions right now . . ." I took one last look down the list, while Rob leaned back in his chair and looked out the window.

"Well," he said, turning back to me, "save your questions if you have any. I think someone has arrived who can answer them better than I can."

In spite of myself, I felt the returning pinch of nerves. "Who?"

"Your roommate. Unless memory fails me, that was her parents' car driving away. She must have been moving into your room while we were talking."

I tried to smile back, bit my lip instead. "What can you tell me about her? I don't even know her name."

"Arianwen Gruffydd," Rod said slowly, and I memorized the pronunciation: ah-ree-AHN-wen GRUF-uth. "An excellent young woman. She's twenty years old, in her third year here. She's about your size, petite, and her hair is about your color, too, chestnut brown, but without the red highlights. Fortunately for you she's a native Welsh speaker, and I'm sure she'll be glad to help you when you start learning. What else? I've forgotten what her "main" is— that's what they say here instead of a college "major." But she's very smart and a fun person. I'm sure you two will get along just fine."

I squinted; the sunlight was very bright, as I stepped out of the Academic Building. I paused on the step and looked at my watch. Almost dinnertime . . . no, "dinner" at home was "supper" here, and "lunch" at home was "dinner" here . . .! So much to remember! Okay, so it was almost *supper*time. I toyed with the idea of going straight to the canteen, then chided myself for being cowardly and set off briskly for the hostel. Everything would be much easier once the roommate was met and conquered!

Laney walked out of the hostel, swinging a tennis racquet. "Well, Morfa Owen! What's up, chick? How did the meeting with Robert go?"

"Just fine! I got into all the classes I wanted. Where are you going? Have you had supper?"

"Yeah. I thought about waiting for you, but I saw your roomie arriving and figured that you'd want a chance to meet her. Anyway, I'm off now to strike the first blow for Equal Rights!" She grinned and brandished the racquet like a sword.

"What in the world are you talking about?"

"Well. I ate lunch—oh, excuse me, dinner—with a

rather dashing young Welshman named Steffan Williams. The Welsh students on the orientation committee are arriving, that's why your roommate is here. Anyway, we talked along fine for a while, after I got used to fighting my way through his accent. Then, for some reason, tennis came up, and he made the incredible suggestion that men players are superior to women players! As former Champion of the Berkeley Junior Tennis League," and she drew herself up grandly, "I felt it was my duty to challenge him to a match to prove once and for all that it's the training and the practice, not the sex, that makes the best tennis player!"

I laughed at her. "Did you find out first whether he was the Aberystwyth Junior League Champion?"

"Um . . . well. Keep your fingers crossed! Are you going down to the pubs tonight?"

"Are you?"

"It's on the orientation schedule. 'Cultural orientation in the pubs with newly arrived Welsh students.' Ha! I get the feeling that we're going to be able to do pretty much as we please around here. The winner of my little upcoming match is buying the loser's first drink."

"Oho, that's the plan is it? And the second drink?"

"You catch on quickly, my dark-haired friend. The activity for tonight on *my* orientation list is 'find and rope into willing servitude a handsome Welsh male.' Phase One is only moments away. Have fun with your roommate!"

"Good luck, and I'll see you tonight!"

"Right-o!" Laney waved and trotted off toward the courts.

I walked into the hostel, feeling very amused by my new friend, and headed for my room quickly before the apprehension about meeting my roommate could return.

Stifling an urge to knock on my own door, I pushed it open gently and peered in. There was no one to be seen, but from the far side of the partition came the sound of running water. I stepped inside, and a high, accented voice called, "Rhys?"

I cleared my throat. "No, it's Morfa Owen, your roommate."

"Morfa!" And around the partition came Arianwen, smiling and drying her hands on a fluffy yellow towel.

"I'd shake hands, but as you can see they're all wet. I'm glad to meet you!"

"Me, too. I mean I'm glad to meet *you!*" Arianwen tossed the towel onto her bed and we shook hands warmly. "Is that side of the room all right with you? I wouldn't mind switching if you want to; I just put my things down in the closest place when I moved in . . ."

"The inside is fine," Arianwen said reassuringly. "I like the view out of that window. Let me go and put this towel away. Then we'll sit down and have a chat, is it?"

Arianwen was very easy to talk to. In the next hour, I told her about my brothers and sister, about my parents and the Airedales and what living in Missouri was like. I described my high school and the things we had done there. Arianwen had never flown, so I described Ireland and England from the air, and how it felt when the plane took off and landed. And she laughed when I told her about my whirlwind experiences with the London train and Underground systems.

When her turn came to talk, it was her accent—soft and lilting—that I paid as much attention to as her words. The way she said some words in a short, clipped way and lengthened others created a dreamy singsong that was almost like listening to poetry. Arianwen was one of three children; she had an older and a younger brother. Rhisiart, the older, was married and lived with his family in Swansea, and Huw, the younger, was just starting school in Bangor, a northern Welsh town. Their parents lived in Dolgellau; Arianwen pronounced it dol-GEH-thlai. That was in the north, too, she explained, and very near the sea. Her family had an old male collie named Tegid. Arianwen's main was education; she planned to teach "infants' school," which I gathered meant grade school. She was in the three-year program at Carmarthen College, so this would be her last year.

"So I want to do everything this year, you know? I'll be on the darts team and the field hockey team, as I was last term. We don't win many matches, but we have a glorious time. I'll have difficult lectures, I'm sure, but there's always time to go down to town in the evening for a pint."

I wasn't quite sure what she meant, but didn't ask because something more interesting had come to mind.

"Who is Rhys?" I tried to pronounce it as Arianwen had, with a breathy "h" at the beginning and a rolled "r," so the whole thing came out as "Hrrees."

"Ah, I'd almost forgotten him! He's my boyfriend. We began going out together when we were First-years. You'll seet him at supper . . . he's very nice, for a bloke. Shall we go down to the canteen?"

"Sure. Just let me run down to the washroom for a minute."

I jumped down the half-flight of stairs in an ecstasy of relief. My roommate was friendly, intelligent, pretty—I liked her, but better yet, she seemed to like me! I had met a Welsh person a little older than me and found that I could understand her, we shared a sense of humor, we could be friends. I even looked forward to meeting Rhys.

Arianwen met me at the door to our room, meal ticket in hand; but she raised her eyebrows at me and gave a quizzical little frown-smile. "Come here, you," and she pulled me by the elbow over to the wardrobe. Our faces were reflected side by side in the mirror on the door, and she said, "Look at that. Strange, is it? I never had a sister, but if I had, she couldn't look more like me than you do."

It was hard for me to see at first, but slowly I realized that she was right. It was more than what Rob had already mentioned: the similarity in our heights and builds, and the texture and color of our hair. It's in the bones too, I thought: we shared high cheekbones, slender noses, and short, clear jawlines. There were certainly differences: besides the red in my hair that Arianwen lacked, my eyes were hazel and hers dark blue, our mouths were shaped differently, her face was slightly longer and thinner than mine. We weren't going to be mistaken for one another, anyway; well, at least not during the daytime.

Arianwen had a different idea.

"Now we've got to work on a Welsh accent for you and get you some sunglasses by next week."

"But why?"

"So you can go to lectures for me, of course!"

The canteen was still far from full. But when I had been there last, there had been one tight knot of American students in the center, all eating together with their talk echoing. Now that the Welsh student orientation committee had arrived, there were smaller, scattered knots all throughout the big, low-ceilinged room, and the echo had fled completely.

Arianwen and I exhibited our meal tickets for the lady in starched white behind the counter and were given cracked brown wooden trays and sets of silverware. We moved down the food aisle together, pointing out our choices to men and women who ladled portions into stoneware bowls and shoved them across the counter. Stoneware cups and tall white tanks full of coffee and tea sat at the end of the aisle. We both chose tea, then moved on to an empty end of one of the long tables.

I looked at Arianwen, then around. "Don't you have some friends you want to sit with? I don't mind," I said, though actually I didn't really feel up to a whole new sea of Welsh faces just yet. Rhys would be enough to start with.

"Na." Arianwen shook her head and sat down, and I settled across from her. "I've known that lot for years. I can talk to them later. Right now I'd rather talk to you—we're only just starting to get to know each other."

The food wasn't terrific, but it was tolerable. I barely noticed it as Arianwen and I fell into conversation again. We felt similarly on a lot of issues, it seemed, though there were things I was terribly anxious to find out about that I just didn't feel comfortable bringing up yet. Politics, for instance. The politics of a small country within a large, dominant one. The subject made a small appearance all on its own, however, when I wasn't expecting it. Arianwen asked me what classes I was taking.

"Well, I have two history courses: one on the Celts, which is a general sort of thing covering Celtic people all over Europe, and one called 'Carmarthen and the Surrounding Communities.' I'm not sure what that covers, but I want to know more about this area."

"Malcolm Davies takes that lecture. That will be good, he knows all about local history. He's to be the guide for tomorrow's walking tour, so you'll see him then."

I slowly realized that Arianwen was talking about a professor, not a student. "Taking" a class at home meant being enrolled in it, but here it evidently meant teaching it!

"What else?"

"Ah, harp lessons, I guess."

"Get away! Really?"

I laughed. "An American friend of mine got me into that one. I've never played the harp in my life. My other two classes are a creative writing tutorial and Welsh for Beginners. I hate to break it to you, but Rob committed you to helping me with my Welsh. I hope you don't mind."

Arianwen stared until I wondered if I had committed some terrible *faux pas*. "Well, what's wrong?" I finally asked sharply.

"Not wrong . . . why in the world would an American want to learn Welsh?"

I wondered uneasily if this was the forerunner of admiration or criticism. "Well, I'm half-Welsh. My mam was brought up in Trevaughan . . ."

"That's just the next town over!"

"I know. I want to go there sometime soon and take a look around. Anyway, she and my aunt moved to the States when they were still young, about our age. My brothers and sister and I have grown up on stories of Wales. That's why I'm here, really, and that's why I have a Welsh name, and why I'm specially interested in the language and history too. It's a beautiful language, and the country has had such a fascinating history." Then, because Arianwen was still staring, I added, a little annoyed, "Why? Does it bother you?"

She shook her head quickly. "Of course not." She smiled apologetically and put a hand on my arm. "I'm sorry to be so rude. I'm just surprised. Stupid of me, really. People study French when they are in France and German in Germany, don't they? But you don't have to know Welsh to get along here—"

"I *want* to," I said firmly. "Even if I didn't like languages, which I do, I'd feel obligated. It's part of my own personal history, isn't it? It always embarrassed me that Mam didn't speak Welsh. And she lived here! I think it's terrible that eighty percent of the people who live here now don't care enough about their history to learn their own language! How can they live with themselves and call themselves Welsh? They're nothing but English, as far as I'm concerned! I—"

I stopped, horrified at myself. Not two hours after meeting my roommate, I might well have just alienated her for the rest of the year, blowing off like that about Arianwen's own country, probably her own friends and family!

But Arianwen was smiling.

"Wel, wel, wel. A fynno barch bid gadarn."

I smiled back tentatively. "Hey, no fair. I haven't even had one Welsh class yet."

She reached across the table and patted my hand. "No matter. I am pleased and impressed. *And* I'll be glad to help you with your Welsh! Very glad. You'll be joining the Language Society yet."

"A language society?" I laughed. "I don't think I can become that fluent in a year!"

Arianwen smiled and shook her head. "The Language Society is something different. I'll tell you about it later, it's too complicated for now. I was joking, anyway. I think."

"Joking about what?"

We both jumped, and the newcomer behind Arianwen's chair laughed.

"Rhys! You daft bat, you nearly scared the life out of me! Sit down."

"Esgusodwch fi, cariad," said Rhys cheerfully, kissing the top of her head and pulling out the chair beside hers.

I glanced at Rhys quickly, then forgot to be polite and

stared. If all Welshmen look like this, I thought, I may have to take some Laney-type action myself!

A thick, dark mane of hair, and a short, thick beard; light blue eyes and dark, expressive brows; short and stocky, but athletic-looking. The word "medieval" kept coming to my mind, and I could much more easily imagine him striding around a Roman British town than in and out of shops or the post office. He looked like the sort of person who was always in a good mood, always anxious to help make others comfortable. But I had a sudden intuitive feeling that if he ever got angry, it would be a fierce, intense anger that came from the deep, uncivilized emotions of another age.

"Rhys, this is my American roommate, Morfa Owen. Morfa, this is Rhys Jones."

Rhys, having just sat down, popped up again and reached for my hand. Shaking it firmly, he smiled warmly and said, "Morfa, croeso! That means 'welcome.' It's good to meet you."

"Thank you. It's great to meet you, too."

Rhys sat down again. Arianwen turned to him and said, "Rhys, Morfa is going to be learning Welsh while she's here! I've promised her our help."

"Well! I'll be glad to help, wrth gwrs." This sounded enough like the English "of course" that I didn't need to ask for a translation. Rhys smiled at me and said, "Shall we begin now?"

"Now?" I was startled.

"Why not? You're going on the pub crawl with us tonight, is it? Arian, you've invited her?"

"Not yet, you burst upon us before I could! You will, won't you, Morfa?"

"Sure, thanks!" I didn't have the slightest idea of what

they were talking about, except that it involved pubs in some way, but I was game for anything.

"Then, how about something to say to the new Welsh students you'll be meeting? Can you say, 'Shw mae'?"

"Shoo my," I repeated carefully, and Rhys and Arianwen applauded.

"Da iawn! 'Shw mae' means 'hello'; it's a short form, like 'hi.' And now, for when we leave them, say, 'Nos da.'"

"Nos da."

"That means 'good night.' See, you're speaking Welsh already! And I bet you thought it would be difficult!"

We all laughed. "I'm sure it is just a bit more difficult than that! But it makes me feel better about it, thanks. I certainly fell into the right hands!"

Rhys and Arianwen smiled, and Arianwen said, "Get away, you! You'll be telling us to shove off in a week."

This was so absurd that I just laughed. Rhys wolfed down his supper, while Arianwen and I talked and joked. When he finished, all three of us took our dirty dishes to the kitchen and stacked them. Arianwen turned to Rhys and said, "Ble mae Gareth?"

"Yn y dre."

"He's going on crawl tonight, is it?"

"Wrth gwrs!" Rhys smiled and turned to me. "Shall we go to the Union for a bit?"

I looked at Arianwen; she smiled and shrugged, leaving it up to me. I gathered my courage and said, "Wrth gwrs!"

Rhys gave a big, booming laugh of appreciation and threw an arm around each of our shoulders. As we left the canteen, he began to sing in Welsh.

4 🦎

Pub Crawl

Hands stuffed deep into my jacket pockets, I leaned back to stare up at the faded wooden horse swinging slowly back and forth above the dimly lit pub door. Beyond the horse, the black sky was splashed with stars, and somehow the snappy breeze that blew seemed to come sweeping straight down from the stars themselves.

The words beneath the horse were faded and were, of course, in Welsh. "Y Ceffyl Du," said Arianwen slowly. "It means 'The Black Horse.'"

"Uh KEFF-ul DEE," I repeated, and she and Rhys nodded, smiling. "It may not seem like much to you, just to be able to repeat Welsh when we speak it," said Rhys, "but it's not easy. You have a good accent."

I smiled and hunched my shoulders, from the cold and embarrassed pleasure.

"'The Ceff' is our favorite pub," said Arianwen, holding the door open and motioning me in. "I'm not sure why, really. It has no jukebox, so there's no music, but a lot of us sing, sometimes. It's small but very friendly. We always start or end our crawls here, or both."

A "pub crawl," I had learned earlier that evening, was sort of like American "bar-hopping," except that the flavor of the thing was different. The point wasn't to get drunk, and it wasn't really even to meet people or pick up members of the opposite sex (though all of this usually became part of a crawl!). It was more a sort of social outing; groups of friends meeting up with one another on crawl, buying each other pints of ale, talking, singing, playing music in the pubs with jukeboxes. Each group of friends had their favorite route of pubs; there was plenty of choice, as Carmarthen had fifty-six pubs in all! And that was the other reason for frequent crawls. There was little else to do at night. The town had one movie theater, and as far as I could tell every single establishment except the pubs, the theater, and two Chinese restaurants closed at five o'clock! The Chinese restaurants were crowded after the pubs closed at 10:30.

We had barely begun to push our way through the mob of people in the Ceff's entrance hall when Rhys was tackled by a group of boys in plaid shirts and jeans. They did an excellent job of pummeling him while holding their glasses upright!

"Rhys, mun!" "Shw mae, ya old waster!" "Let's get you a pint, mun!" and they dragged him, laughing and protesting, into one of the Ceff's side rooms where their shouts for service could be heard even over the din.

"And that's the last we'll see of *him* for a bit!" Arianwen grinned at me and shrugged. "He hasn't seen most of his mates all summer. Here," and she began to weave through the crowd into the main room, as I followed closely behind. Near the middle of the room we stopped, and I stared around me, dazed. Arianwen laughed and said, "What'll it be? First pint's on me."

"I don't even know what there is! Aren't you supposed to drink ale or something like that?"

"You could do. There's better, though."

"Bring me whatever you like best, okay?"

"Right. Ta-ta!" And she turned and began to push her way toward the bar. I began to scrutinize the Ceff.

The main room was big enough to hold a crowd, but small enough to require mingling. There was a piano across the room, a dartboard, a long bar, tables with stools and benches around the walls, and people everywhere! Men from town formed a ring around the bar, sitting on tall stools, drinking dark ale and talking gravely among themselves. Students lounged on the benches, laughing uproariously over some joke in one corner, arguing over who was to buy the next round in another. A group of Welsh students played darts at the far end of the room. And knots of people stood all over the floor, packed so closely together that the only way you could tell who was with whom was by which way they were facing!

Talk was loud but cheerful, people gesturing with a free hand between gulps from tall pint glasses. I searched out Arianwen, who was at the bar being served by a small, smiling man in a white smock. I glanced around the room again. Someone at the arguing table got up and moved to the bar, having been drafted to buy for the group. The laughing table was laughing even harder! I wondered how long they had been there. Arianwen had told me that pub crawls often began at about six o'clock, and it was almost nine now. The darts game had finished, and the winner was being congratulated. He gave a deep mock bow and nodded, evidently accepting his former opponents' offer of a celebratory drink. He was handsome, this fellow. I watched him walk to the bar and decided that he probably knew it all too well. Dusty blond hair fell to his eyes, which appeared to be light green or gray. His build was slender and athletic-looking. The most impressive features were his high cheekbones and deep-set eyes, giving him a spirited, almost startled look. Then suddenly *I* became the one with the startled look, as a cold beer glass attached itself to my arm.

"Wake up, you!" Arianwen laughed and thrust a glass of clear amber liquid at me. "Don't worry, you'll soon get used to this place. Here."

"What is this?" It smelled like apple cider.

"It's cider," said Arianwen. "Strongbow. Try it."

"What, no alcohol? I know, you think Americans are lightweights." I laughed and took a deep drink. Then I stopped and stared at Arianwen. Then at the cider. I took another drink.

It was very, very good. But this wasn't like the cider they had in Missouri.

Arianwen burst into laughter. "I hope you can hold your pints! Cider is more alcoholic than lager. Tastes better too, is it?"

I nodded vigorously. "It's great! Like cider at home, but with a kick. We don't have this in the States at all, I don't think." I took another drink.

"So what do you think of the Ceff?"

"I love it! What a fun place. This is your regular pub?"

Arianwen nodded. "There are some others that we like . . . Jackson's. The Guelder Rose. But this is our favorite. Sorry there's nowhere to sit. You have to get here by seven to get a table."

"No, I like standing out here watching everyone. And speaking of everyone, that reminds me. Do you know a Welsh student named Steffan Williams?"

"Steff? Ya! He's a Second-year. Good bloke. He lives one room down from Rhys in Dewi Hostel. You've met him then, is it?"

"No, but my American friend Laney had a tennis match

with him this afternoon, and whoever won was to buy the loser a beer in the pubs tonight."

"That'll be in the Guelder Rose. Steff comes here sometimes, but usually goes there. We'll collect Rhys and go there to hunt for them after we finish our pints."

"We don't have to—"

"That's all right! What's a crawl if you stay at one pub all night? The Guelder Rose is next anyway. We were hoping to find Rhys's friend Gareth Efans here before we went on. He arrived late this morning and had things to do in town all day."

"I remember hearing you mention his name to Rhys at supper . . ."

"That's right. The three of us are kind of best mates; we do a lot together. You'll like him, I think. If he ever shows up! He's probably lost." She laughed.

As people pushed their way to and from the bar, Arianwen identified them for me and told me a little about each of them. Finally I said, "Is there anyone in Carmarthen you don't know?"

She smiled. "Lots of the townies. I know everyone from college but some of the new First-years. Everybody knows everybody all over Wales, almost. It's nice, isn't it?" Before I could answer, Arianwen glanced over my head and a smile broke across her face. "There—hey, Gareth!" She pushed past me toward the bar and the group of darts players. I had a sudden, belated premonition about who "Gareth" was, and I was right. The winner of the darts match turned and caught Arianwen up in a hug.

"Arian! Shw mae, cariad!" A torrent of Welsh followed that was totally over my head. I walked up slowly behind Arianwen, absurdly embarrassed, feeling as if I had been caught watching him play darts. As if anyone would care!

As if anyone had seen me. Maybe I was just nervous because Gareth was so detached-looking. I felt terribly, awkwardly *American* . . .

Arianwen turned and made a gesture that included me in the group. "This is my American roommate, Morfa Owen," she said. "Morfa, this is Gareth Efans."

Gareth turned his pale green, assessing eyes on me and nodded with such solemn politeness that I became annoyed. I gathered my courage and said coolly, "Gareth, shw mae, mun."

His eyes widened suddenly and he opened his mouth to speak when he was pounced on from behind.

"Gareth, mun! You old dog. Where have you been keeping, twpsyn?" Rhys squeezed his friend, then released him so that he could punch him in the back. Gareth grinned, evidently used to this treatment, and pinched Rhys's nose.

"Rhys. Faint o'r gloch yw hi?"

Rhys looked at his watch. "Half past nine. Where now?"

Arianwen said, "Steff's in the Guelder Rose."

Rhys clapped Gareth on the back. "We're off, then. You can buy me a pint there for being late."

Gareth laughed and protested in Welsh as Rhys herded him and Arianwen guided me through the crowd toward the door. We shoved our glasses between bodies onto the bar on our way out, where we stepped onto cobbles shiny and slick from a sudden rain.

Rhys bounced along in great spirits, talking away to Gareth who smiled and nodded occasionally in return. Arianwen and I walked behind, hunched slightly against the mist falling around us. I looked from my friends to Gareth and back again, trying to understand what the attraction was. He seemed much too solemn and haughty for my outgoing friends. There must be more to him than there appears to be, I decided. Don't judge too quickly. This *is* a foreign country, after all. And Gareth's accent seemed much thicker than Rhys's or Arianwen's. Perhaps he was just from a smaller town, less used to meeting people.

The last thing I needed to do was take a dislike to Rhys's and Arianwen's best friend.

As soon as we arrived at the Guelder Rose, I was sent off to make jukebox selections while the others hunted for Steffan and Laney. The Guelder Rose was as crowded as the Ceff had been. I pushed my way through the mob to the jukebox and enjoyed the feel of the heavy British coins before dropping them in the slot. I turned the dial that made the song titles flip over . . . then jumped as a low, accented voice at my shoulder asked quietly, "What d'ya think of the IRA?"

Gareth's voice. I paused, fingers on knob, taken completely off guard. Why had he come away from the others? Panic began to rise as I realized that I couldn't remember what the IRA was! The first thing that came to mind was annual tax returns, but no, that was the IRS. And then it came to me . . . the Irish Republican Army.

I turned slowly to face the icy green eyes, wondering what to answer. It was such a hot issue, and I didn't know yet whether the Welsh sympathized with the Irish or the English.

Then I remembered that I didn't care what he thought of me and decided on the truth.

"Well, I agree with their philosophy, but not with their methods."

Gareth's intent look changed a little, inscrutably, then became a slight smile. Despite not caring what he thought, my heart began to pound with relief. Two narrow escapes in one day! How often did politics come up around here, anyway? I'd surely be out of luck before long, at this rate.

Afraid to risk discussing a subject I knew so little about, I held out my hand and said, "I'm glad to meet you. Our introduction was interrupted . . ."

He nodded and shook hands gravely. "Gareth Efans," he said, pronouncing the 'f' in 'Efans' like a 'v,' the same as in 'Morfa.' "Oedd, nac oedd. Mae Rhys yn ddiawl digywylydd. Wyt ti wedi bod yma'n hir te? Ti'n siarod Cymraeg . . ."

I stared, dumbfounded. Was this some kind of joke? But then he looked puzzled, too, and said, "You're a Welsh-speaker, no?"

Light dawning, I had to cover my mouth to keep from shouting with laughter. So my little joke at the Ceff had worked! "No, no, no! Well, about five words. I can say 'Shw mae' and 'Nos da' . . . does 'mun' count? Rhys taught me that much this evening. I *am* taking Welsh class when school begins, though . . ."

Gareth shook his head, smiling ruefully, and gave the same little mock bow he had given at the end of the darts match. "Excuse me, then! Your accent is good. What I said was yes, our introduction was interrupted, and that Rhys is a rude devil, but maybe that's me, is it? And I asked if you've been here long because you speak Welsh . . ."

"I arrived yesterday, and it's the first time I've been out of the States at all. Do you want to help me decide on music?" I asked suddenly, no longer overwhelmed by him. He looked a little surprised, then half-smiled, shrugged and said "Aye." We looked through the selection, a good part of which was either American songs I was familiar with, or songs I didn't know by British bands. A table emptied just as we used our last coin, and we grabbed it and sat down. Gareth had just turned to me and said, "Why did you come to Wales?" when Rhys and Arianwen came pushing through the crowd with drinks in hand. Laney followed them, accompanied by a small, wiry dark Welshman who must be Steffan. He looked as much like a dark elf as Laney did a blonde one, with mischievous blue eyes and a crooked smile. He wore a black leather jacket and jeans with holes in the knees. Laney introduced us; he shook hands vigorously and said an enthusiastic "Hiya" before attacking Gareth, who fended him off, laughing. Laney plunked down beside me, giving Gareth an appreciative stare.

"My God, Morfa Owen, is that *yours*?"

I blushed, to my embarrassment, and said, "Of course not! That's Gareth Efans, a friend of Rhys's and Arianwen's."

"He looks like a Welsh prince."

"He's arrogant enough."

"Hm." Laney nodded. "I believe it. Look at those eyes! He reminds me a little of Michael York in *The Three Musketeers*. Same haughty look. If you decide you don't want him, let me know, okay?"

I laughed. "Be my guest! Steff looks like he'd be more fun, though. Which reminds me, who won the tennis match?"

Laney looked up and whistled. To my tremendous amusement, Steff left Gareth and came over immediately.

Laney drained the last drop from her glass and held it out imperiously. "Fetch me another." Steff grimaced as Rhys and Gareth laughed. Then he shrugged, resigned, and pushed toward the bar with her glass!

She gave me a long sliding glance and shrugged. "It's

all in the training," she said with a yawn and dancing eyes.

We left the Guelder Rose reluctantly when it closed at 10:30. After a short walk around the dark and emptying town, Rhys suggested we make it an early night.

"After all, we've only just arrived. We could all use some extra sleep."

"Let's do go back up to coll," said Arianwen, using the usual abbreviation for college, "and if we aren't tired we can all have coffee in our room, is it?" She looked at me questioningly and I said, "Sure," so that's what we decided on.

As we headed up Glannant Road, I noticed that there was a slight ground fog rising. The rain had completely stopped while we were in the second pub, and the sky was clear and full of stars again. But as I looked around, I saw gray wisps of fog floating over the tops of the stone walls that enclosed the road. It seemed a little odd for such a clear night, but no one else mentioned it. Arianwen and Gareth were walking ahead, talking seriously in Welsh. Rhys was telling Laney, Steff and me about the playwriting workshop he had attended during the summer. And then I was suddenly aware of a small but irritating pebble in my shoe.

I stopped, calling to the others that I would catch right up with them. I sat on the low curb, took off my shoe and shook it upside down. A stone fell out and rolled into a grating. As I slipped my foot back into the shoe and tied it, I heard slow footsteps coming toward me from the direction in which my friends had gone. Looking up, expecting to see one of them returning for me, I saw instead only a thick, light gray blanket of fog! Alarmed at how quickly it had rolled in, and at how unfamiliar I was with the tiny road I was on, I jumped up and called, "Rhys? Laney? Hey, is that you guys?"

There was no answer, and no pause in the footfalls. Afraid, suddenly, for no reason, I backed up against the stone wall, wet and clammy against my shirt. A breeze swirled bits of fog around eerily, until the footsteps were upon me and the fog parted to reveal an unfamiliar face.

He wasn't close enough to touch, but about halfway across the street. Fog floated gently around the figure, making him seem vague and unearthly. He appeared to be about thirty years old, with a thick beard and long dark hair that brushed the top of his turned-up collar. A long dark coat swirled around him as he walked, so deeply involved with his thoughts that it seemed as if they weighed on him, slowed him down. It struck me that he was struggling with some terrible problem, and while I was still afraid, I felt sorry for him. He looked dangerous, but not evil.

Suddenly I turned and ran blindly up the road after my friends. Almost immediately the fog thinned, and when they appeared not far ahead at all, it was almost gone. They had stopped to wait for me and exclaimed when they saw me. I must be a strange sight, I thought ruefully, running terrified out of a fog. I knew I was shaking.

"Morfa! What happened?"

Rhys took my arm and looked sternly into my face. "Are you all right?"

I nodded, trying to smile, to reassure him. "I'm sorry. It's a silly thing . . . did you see a man in a long coat pass by just a few seconds ago?"

They looked at each other, shrugging and shaking their heads.

"There was no one here but us."

I was incredulous, and fear came creeping back. "You're kidding! But he *must* have passed by here! Unless you missed him in the fog—" I stopped as they looked at each

other again, eyebrows raised. I turned and looked behind
me.

The road was clear.

Rhys put an arm around me. "Hey. I bet I know what
happened. You sat down to get the rock out of your shoe,
and a man walked past suddenly and startled you. He
might have come out of one of the houses around here or
from down a side street, so we would have missed him.
Sometimes when you're frightened suddenly, everything
else goes blank around you. That happened and you
thought it was fog. There, isn't that probably it?"

I felt a little, hesitant relief. But hadn't I seen the fog
for several minutes before I felt the rock in my shoe? Well,
maybe I had just imagined it. Maybe . . .

"That's probably what happened . . ."

"Well, then!" Everyone smiled and turned to head on
up the road, Laney walking by me and chatting lightly,
Gareth turning once to smile encouragingly at me. The fear
passed and as the memory faded, I began to really believe
that I had imagined the entire thing. When we reached
the college, I was as anxious as the rest to have a little
party in our room before bed. And it was a lot of fun; even
Gareth loosened up a little.

But when I woke the next morning, it was with the
uneasy feeling that the strange, dark man had spent the
night walking in my dreams.

5 🦎

St. Peter's of Carmarthen

It was a perfect day for a walking tour of Carmarthen, the activity on the orientation list. The sun was bright, but a breeze blew cool and refreshing. Trees and grass surrounding the walk between the hostels shone greenly brilliant, with no sign of autumn in them yet.

The American students gathered in the History room to wait for the professor who was to conduct our tour, Malcolm Davies. Laney arrived last, bouncing through the doorway, pausing to exchange some laughing comment with Lisa Braddock and Jim McNae, then walking over to me. She grinned a hello and turned to hop up onto a desk.

"So how are you this morning? Seen D'Artagnan since sunrise?"

I blushed and gave her a half-amused, half-exasperated glare, but before I could say anything the door slammed and everyone fell silent.

A short, square man stood in front of the still trembling door. His face was that of a Disney troll. He glared at us with fierce bright eyes, from under full, bushy brows. Then an amazing contortion took place. The brows shot up and jaw dropped simultaneously; then, ever so slowly, the eyebrows came down until they narrowed the eyes below them into slits, the jaw rose until the mouth was nearly pressed against the nose . . . it was as if his features were flowers in a fiercely squeezed bouquet! Laney poked me repeatedly in the ribs until I was in agony trying to keep from laughing at this very odd man.

Thoroughly scrutinized, we evidently were accepted. Brows relaxed and mouth smiled cheerfully as Dr. Davies addressed us for the first time.

"So! Tiny tots! Coming on my walking tour, are we?" His accent popped his words about; it made me think of cartoons I had seen as a child that taught preschoolers to read by bouncing a ball on top of each syllable. "V-e-r-y brave tots! Not afraid, are we?" He dropped so suddenly into a hunched position that I just caught myself in time to keep from doing it too, and some of the others *did* drop! "Fall into the gratings you will! That happened last term. Lost all our Americans through the gratings in the streets! Tiny American tots wandering underground for years and years; and now we're willing to try it again, is it?" He popped upright. "Well, well, well, well, WELL!"

On that last "well," Dr. Davies pirouetted and plunged out of the room, slamming the door behind him.

For a few moments, we stared at each other. We weren't sure whether to laugh, worry, or take the next train back to London! Laney opened her mouth to speak, but then there was a muffled shout from the parking lot visible through the big glass windows behind us. We turned to look.

It was Dr. Davies, beaming and jumping up and down like an excited two-year-old. He cupped his hands around his mouth as if we were a mile away and shouted, "Tots! are we lost already then? Come out *here,* like a good lot!"

We straggled down Glannant Road toward Carmarthen behind the effusive Dr. Davies, who bounced and sang boomingly in Welsh. The road couldn't look more different than it had last night, I thought with a shiver as we turned the corner where I had stopped to shake the stone out of my shoe. I glanced around quickly, half-fearing another glimpse of the dark man, or another fog, before reminding myself that I had imagined the whole thing. It was easier today, to believe that I had imagined it.

"What's your roommate doing this morning?" asked Laney, balancing on the edge of the curb.

"Sleeping in, the lazy thing! Um, she and Rhys and the other Student Guides have a meeting later this morning, with Rob, I guess. They'll be out in time for lunch—I mean dinner."

"Hm. Well, Steff—and Gareth, just in case you're interested—has a soccer club meeting this morning with some of the other Welsh students. Only they call it football, not soccer. Rhys doesn't play, does he?"

"No, he plays rugby. Why do you keep telling me what Gareth's doing? I told you last night that as far as I'm concerned, he's all yours."

Laney shook her head and smiled a little twisted Steffan-smile. "That may be true as far as *you're* concerned, my dear. But I have a funny feeling about the two of you. And as far as *I'm* concerned, I think I'm better off with Steff. He's exactly what I'm looking for; someone to play with, if you know what I mean. Your Welsh prince is far too serious for me. And once you got in with him, it wouldn't be easy to pull out again. I plan to have the time of my life here and then break clean. And Gareth is a Nationalist, you know . . ."

"So is Steffan, isn't he?"

Laney shook her head. "No."

"He speaks Welsh, I heard him!"

"I know. But he and I talked about that a little last night. Being a Welsh-speaker and being a Nationalist are two different things. You can speak Welsh and still be a happy British citizen. But the Nationalists, they want Wales to be free from England altogether. I don't think I'd want to get involved with a Nationalist. It'll be fun having them as friends; different points of view and all. But a boyfriend? I want his main interest to be *me,* not politics. Isn't he good-looking, though! So is Rhys, for that matter. And a poet into the bargain! What did you think of the stuff he read us last night?"

"Great, wasn't it?" I nodded appreciatively. "And terribly mystical. But did you notice Arianwen when he was reading it?"

Laney glanced at me. "Didn't seem very thrilled, did she?"

I shook my head. "No, not at all. When he said that it was the best thing he had done all summer, I thought she was going to get up and walk out of the room!"

"He didn't notice, though."

"No, luckily his back was to her then."

"But Gareth noticed, did you see?"

"No, did he? That doesn't surprise me, though. He seems like the sort who would always be aware of everything."

Laney shrugged and ran her hand along the stones in the wall. "Well, *I* liked it! We can start a Rhys Jones Appreciation Society ourselves!"

We laughed and looked around as we entered the sunlit town. The walking tour began near the center of Carmarthen, on Lammas Street.

It didn't take me long to decide that Dr. Davies had either been acting silly earlier to help us relax, or he was the best kind of eccentric. He certainly wasn't stupid. His descriptions of the town in different stages of history as we walked along were marvelous; we felt we could see the town change around us. He spoke of when there was a medieval town where Carmarthen stood and strode around describing the tall stone walls that were used for defense, the monastary at the town gate. The old gate was long gone, but it had stood where there was now a street called—Dark Gate! He explained the history of more of the street names, the political rivalry between the "Red" and "Blue" factions several hundred yearrs ago, so that now the street cutting the town in half was called Red Street from the center of the town eastward, and Blue Street from. the center on west!

Slowly he went further back in history. We walked along the cobbled streets until we came to a section of town that I remembered from my first mini-bus ride up from the train station. A little church sat surrounded by a circular graveyard, within a circle of road, and across from it lay a large parking lot and the public library. We crossed the street and stood in the parking lot (called a "car park," I noticed, looking at the bilingual sign. The Welsh equivalent was "Maes Parcio."). Dr. Davies gestured across the street toward the church.

"This church was built during the Middle Ages. It is of the same materials as the medieval walls and houses. But why did the people of that time build this church? From what I have told you of the structure of the medieval town, you can tell that it was outside the town wall. Outside the only protection those people had, in days when the surrounding forests were full of wolves and robbers. There was great risk in coming outside of those walls. And I showed you where there was a church inside the walls. There were not enough people to fill two churches. Why, then, did they risk their lives to come out here and build this one?"

No one answered. Laney and I exchanged puzzled glances.

"And the old records show that the inhabitants of medieval Carmarthen always came out in force to this church on their most holy days. Why? What made this church the special one?"

Silence.

"And the round graveyard. Why a round one, when the building practices of the time demanded a square one? Why is the graveyard round?"

After a pause, when he clearly had every bit of our attention, Dr. Davies smiled and the tension he had raised eased slightly. "I will tell you, my friends. It is because this was a holy place of holy places. The medievals were not the first to make this place sacred ground, nor to perform their most holy rituals here. Somewhere, far, far back in time, this place was pagan holy ground, and the broken memory filtered down through generations who couldn't remember exactly *why* this place was so special, this little spot of ground on a hill, but they firmly knew that it *was*, so holy building after holy building rose and fell here. Had you noticed that it *is* on a hill? Because that is our one clue to the beginning, our one passport back to the very dawn of civilization and the reason for the hold this spot has had on so many different peoples and religions."

I examined the church and the graveyard. Yes, it was on a hill, but such a gentle one that I hadn't noticed it before. The road that ran around the graveyard sloped slightly upward, and the church was perched on the peak of the little hill.

Dr. Davies' voice was unexpectedly quiet. "It is the remains of a stone circle which raises that hill; a circle of stones long fallen and covered by layers and layers of earth through thousands of years. But it stood here once, almost as big and as proud as Stonehenge. It was the second largest ring of stones in Britain and the second holiest pagan place in Britain. This spot is on a direct magnetic line with Stonehenge. Clearly it was built for some mighty and wondrous purpose, with great effort and dedication and reverence, by the dwellers of prehistoric Britain. That purpose sank beyond even legend and mystery into utter silence long, long ago. But the force that created it has lived on so powerfully that generation after generation of Welsh, totally ignorant of it, honored it even in ignorance."

Chills ran up my arms.

The rest of the lecture was anticlimactic, even when Dr. Davies told us that the car park on which we stood spread over the buried ruins of Maridunum, the Roman Carmarthen. That was exciting, but—the Roman city had risen, lived out its existence and died, period. The hill, though . . . I was silent as Laney and I wandered back toward Glannant Road and the college. The hill, and what lay on it and under it, was proof of some force other than the everyday ones I had always known. Some force that spoke powerfully out of the earth to people of all races and religions, who blindly and reverently obeyed. A force that has always existed . . . a chill returned as the thought struck me: what is that force doing now?

I had asked Dr. Davies the name of the church. It was St. Peter's of Carmarthen. "This time," he had added with a chuckle, and I had realized he meant that the churches there had had many names, and the name didn't really matter at all. In time this church would fall, and in some future time be replaced by some future people who, knowing or unknowing, would obey the same, single-minded power.

I sat at my desk for a long time that afternoon drawing aimlessly and thinking about St. Peter's of Carmarthen.

And thinking seriously for the first time since I was a child that perhaps Ethan and Sheena were right.

Maybe there *was* "magic" in the world.

The week passed in a blur of pleasure for me, as memories of fog and mystical powers faded in the clear, bright realities of everyday life in Wales. My desire not to make American friends was forgotten as Laney took over Sheena's place in my life. If her family was wealthy, as I suspected, she had brought none of it to Wales with her; she appeared in worn-looking jeans and sweat shirts all of the time, wore no make-up, put on no airs. I loved her fresh, frank way of looking at things and her total honesty in dealing with people. You couldn't help but enjoy yourself with her, because she was having such a marvelous time herself! She had come to rebel, to do nothing but what she wanted to do, and she did it with relish. I tried to imagine her life with the socialite Aunt Lou in her San Francisco home, and at school with the Estelle Bingham-Jones crowd, and failed completely. She belonged on a ranch in Colorado, or protesting something at an Eastern university, or on a skin cream commercial!

We explored Carmarthen, and it began to feel like home. We threw Laney's Frisbee on Glannant Road . . . grew tired of that, and climbed the embankment on the far side to race through the pasture, scattering startled cows, until we reached the woods and our secret grotto and flung ourselves down, gasping and laughing . . . we waded through leftover puddles of rain, the hoods of our "macs" thrown back, to the town market on Wednesday and Saturday mornings, to poke through cheeses, haggle over the price of Army surplus trousers, choose posters and knickknacks for our rooms . . . Laney riffled through antique postcards ("Morfa, look!" Astonished giggle. It was a postcard of St.

Cyril's Asylum, located up Glannant Road from Carmarthen College. ("What would you write on this one? 'Wish you were here'?"), while I chatted with the marvelous scarf-and-blanket lady who had a farm near Llandovery and wanted me to come and visit her and her granddaughter some time. And when soccer workouts began, we would buy some wine, cheese and a big loaf of hard bread in town, put it in Laney's backpack and spread out a picnic by the field while we watched the boys play. Steff would come trotting over afterward, sweaty and cheerful and ready for a hunk of bread and swig of wine. Sometimes Gareth wandered over, too, to Laney's delight.

There were a few more planned activities for the Americans during Orientation Week. We made another trip with Malcolm Davies. This one was to the coal valleys of South Wales, riding through ghost town after ghost town in the bus while Dr. Davies gave us such an interesting lecture that we didn't realize it was a lecture at all. And then there was a Folk Night in a little town a long bus ride away. We visited the graveyard there first, with its impressive Celtic cross, cryptic headstone inscriptions and an overgrown path that would have done justice to *Dracula*. Laney and I adored the graveyard, but Arianwen seemed a bit nervous, and we were branded "silly twits" for enjoying it so. Then we went to the Folk Music Festival in a big pub nearby and heard the Welsh national anthem sung for the first time. It was in Welsh and I couldn't understand the words, but it was sung with such feeling that it brought tears to my eyes, and Laney's too, to my surprise. Two groups of folk singers followed, singing lively songs in Welsh that had repeating choruses we could learn to sing with them. Rhys went up front between groups of singers and told what was evidently an extremely funny story in Welsh. Everyone there seemed to know and respect him,

though many of them were local townspeople. For the first
time I began to believe what Arianwen had told me about
everyone in Wales knowing everyone else.

After Rhys's story and before the second group of singers,
Laney and I went outside to sit on the little bridge over a
stream by the pub and talk about everything, from how
we felt about Wales to Charles Williams's books and Rhys's
latest poetry.

If Laney took Sheena's place in my life, I guess that
Rhys took the place of Ethan and Sam, with a little extra
patience and politeness thrown in. Determined to give me
a headstart in my Welsh class, he read every Welsh sign
we saw aloud and made me repeat it over and over again
until I got word, accent and inflection perfect. Sometimes
when he came up to our room looking for Arianwen and
she was out, he would settle into our easy chair and read
me his latest poetry. He never did this when Arianwen
was there. Most of his poems dealt with old Welsh mythol-
ogy and legends, and with mysticism, and I got the feeling that these were touchy subjects between Rhys and
Arianwen. Certainly she was very down-to-earth. We
enjoyed each others' company and spent afternoons wandering through shops downtown or talking about the differences in our cultures. But she would rarely join Laney
and me in our explorations through the nearby fields and
hills and seemed pretty unsure of Laney altogether. I
think that was because she didn't believe in doing anything unconventional, and Laney wasn't interested in anything that *was* conventional! This could hardly count as
a major fault, though; Arianwen was a sweet person and a
great roommate. I felt incredibly lucky in my friends.

Gareth's path and mine crossed fairly often, since he,
Rhys and Steff were such close friends. But not only was

Laney totally wrong about our being "meant for each other" in some way, but we remained only rather distant friends for quite a long time. The turning point in our relationship came one night at a little party in Rhys's room in Dewi Hostel.

I had awakened that morning to an incredible clamor outside my window. Jumping up and opening the curtains, I realized with a painful jolt that this was the day the rest of the Welsh students were scheduled to return to college. And there they were, or the first wave of them at least, coming in the narrow lane with much honking of horns and crowding together of tiny cars, parents helping carry suitcases into the hostels, friends hugging each other and talking in gestures and yelling across the lane at one another as more arrived. Yes, and there were Rhys and Arianwen, laughing and helping unload friends' cars. I didn't see Steff or Gareth though. I let the curtain drop and sat down slowly on the desk chair. What would happen to my friendship with them, now that their Welsh friends were back? It wasn't hard to see how I might very well be pushed further and further away until I was excluded from their lives altogether . . .

But the next thing I knew they were coming into the room, flushed and laughing and eager to tell me about all of their friends who were returning. Rhys had planned a party in his room for that night, so I could meet his friends and they could meet Laney and me.

"They had planned a crawl, wrth gwrs, but they'll do as I say," said Rhys with high-spirited arrogance. "I told them they must meet my new American mates. Then they'll understand why I'll be neglecting them all term!"

"It sounds great," I said, nervous but pleased and reassured.

"No need to fear," said Arianwen, perceptive as always. "After a few pints they'll be so pissed they won't know you're an American!"

"I believe it!" I said, laughing.

Rhys's room couldn't hold them all, of course. Welsh students spilled out all through Dewi's second floor hall, lounging on the hall floor or in one of the other rooms, which were all open. Lamps were switched on here and there instead of overhead lights, which, mixed with the full moonlight through the windows, made a very comfortable dim glow. Each person arrived with a big bottle of cider or ale—or two, or three. I was introduced to Dai and Rhisiart and Siw and Sian and Dewi and Pedr and Rhian and Mair . . . About half greeted me in Welsh and asked me about learning Welsh while I was here, and the other half greeted me in English and didn't mention the language at all. Some seemed to be sizing me up as they smiled and shook hands, some seemed genuinely friendly. Rhys managed to stay comfortingly close, while also being a buoyant host. Arianwen sat by me at first, but drifted off to talk to friends later. After being introduced all round, Laney moved into a corner with Steff and eventually disappeared with him altogether.

Growing restless, I got up and headed down the hall for a look at some of the other rooms in Dewi. I elbowed through the knots of people in the hall, being greeted cordially by some and ignored by others, glancing in doors as I passed. Most of them, like Rhys's, were full of laughing, drinking, chatting Welsh students, but the crowd thinned as I neared the end of the hall away from the staircase. Two doors across from each other were shut; the muffled sound of Laney's laughter trickled out from behind one of them. I smiled and walked past to the last room on the corridor. Its door was half-open and, as open house seemed to be the rule of the day, I peered around the corner into the room.

Bold-print Welsh-language posters covered the walls of the otherwise rather bare room. A few eight by ten black-and-white photographs hung by the closet door, and a small pile of books and a tape player lay on a shelf by the bed, but there was nothing else. Except the occupants, of course. Gareth sat on the brown-blanketed bed, speaking quietly but emphatically to a man probably ten years older, who sat in his desk chair.

Gareth fell silent, and both men glanced quickly at me, annoyed. I flushed and said, "I'm sorry, Gareth, I didn't mean to interrupt you! I was just—" and without bothering to finish my vague excuse I started to back away from the door.

"Morfa!" Annoyance turned slowly to confused surprise, and Gareth waved to me impatiently. "No, come in. Cemlyn was just leaving . . ." This said with a steady gaze toward the older man, and I felt some tension between them. Uneasy, but reluctant to insult him by leaving, I stood in the doorway shifting from foot to foot as Gareth and Cemlyn exchanged a final quick few words in Welsh. Then they both rose, Cemlyn smiling absently at me as he passed through the doorway and strode down the hall.

"Sit down." Gareth passed me to push the door shut as I made my way to the vacated desk chair. "Too loud," he explained, opening a drawer and selecting a tape. He put it in the tape player and pushed the button. After a few seconds, soft rock music in Welsh filled the room. Gareth sat on the bed and looked at me expectantly. I hadn't planned on this at all. I looked around the room, finally locating a poster that I could translate, thanks to Rhys.

"Cymru am byth," I said, pronouncing it as Rhys had taught me, KUM-ree ahm BEETH. "Wales Forever. You're a Nationalist, aren't you?"

Gareth cocked his head, pale green eyes sparkling challengingly. "And what do you know about Nationalists?"

"I know that you want Wales to be free from England; not much else, yet. But I'd like to learn. Tell me about Welsh Nationalists."

The green eyes went dark, and without moving, Gareth seemed to turn inward. "And why? Going to take us up as a charity, is it? Something to amuse the rich Americans?"

"Hey, look. What's your problem? Why can't you answer a question without interrogating me first? And anyway, if you think I'm a rich American, you're nuts."

"Oh." His smile was slow and his voice soft. "And how many cars does your family have?"

I hesitated. "Two . . ."

He nodded. "Ahh. And do you have a washing machine for clothes?"

I nodded. I knew I was falling into his trap, but suddenly I was less angry. I was getting a new perspective on the word "rich."

"And for dishes?"

I nodded again. "All right, Gareth. You've made your point. Quit."

"Very few families here have even one car, and I know none with two. I know one family with a dishwasher, and as for clothes . . ."

I cut him off. "I said, I get your point! You don't have to go on and on about it. But that's not my fault. We live in different economic systems . . ."

"And ours was forced on us!"

"Well, damn it, do you think they asked me if I wanted mine? I didn't have any choice either! If you're going to hold me personally responsible for Americans having enough money so that families can have two cars, we might as well hang it up right now."

He looked over my head at a poster on the wall.

"My family may have two cars, but that doesn't mean I have a lot of money: I *don't*. If I hadn't gotten a scholarship, I wouldn't be here. And if I *could* support your Nationalists, I wouldn't. You can sink or swim by yourselves for all I care. If you're never going to even tell me what they are, I can hardly decide whether I think they're right or not, can I? If they're all as unreasonable as you, they're probably wrong anyway."

He looked at me then, and I glared back at him. He stood suddenly and I cringed slightly, afraid he was going to hit me. It would never happen at home, but here? But he didn't. He walked to the window and stood there, leaning against the sill and staring out at the dark campus.

"We want to be free of England, yes," he said abruptly. "But that isn't the main thing. Home Rule would be brilliant, but it seems that a lot of people aren't ready for that. Instead, we're working to make the language available to more people. Did you know there's almost no Welsh on the telly at all, and what there is is mostly news and the like. Nothing for children . . . so they grow up hearing English and speaking English. We want a Welsh language television station. And more Welsh on the radio, and all schools in Wales bilingual . . . everything bilingual. That's all for now. Home Rule will have to wait."

He turned to me, and the challenge had faded from his eyes. I shrugged and said, "I can't see why everyone in Wales wouldn't want those things."

Garcth smiled ruefully and walked around to sit on the bed again. He leaned forward, pushing the hair from his eyes.

"Only one-fifth of the Welsh speak Welsh. The others think it's too hard and don't want it forced on them. Their own language, forced on them! We are fighting a very hard battle here in our own country, convincing people of the need for Welsh, before we even begin to think about London."

I leaned onto the back legs of the chair, to think better. "I suppose it's still sort of a matter of pride for the English too, isn't it? It would be sort of galling to conquer a country and find that, five hundred years later, they're still speaking their own language!"

Gareth laughed. The tape switched off and he rose to turn it over. "You're right. They don't like us and we don't like them. A magic love affair, is it? You know Cemlyn, the bloke who was here? Well, he's president of the Language Society, for this year. We were arguing a bit . . . I was president last year, and I don't think he's doing enough. Too much talk and not enough action, is it? But it's early yet."

I wondered what sort of action he meant, but decided to ask Rhys later. I wasn't sure how secret this society was and didn't want to ruin Gareth's sudden good humor by asking him too much.

"Coffee?"

"Sure, thanks."

And from that point on there was a new Gareth Efans. The aloofness, the hostility and the challenge disappeared completely and instead he asked about my family and my past life, told me about his own, smiled and laughed and was generally a fun, congenial person. Why the change, I didn't know. Maybe I had passed some strange Nationalist test for foreigners, but how I had done it I had no idea. Gareth translated the rest of his posters for me and we discussed Nationalism and the Welsh Language Society some more before I finally left his room at a quarter after three! I groaned as I looked at my watch.

"And I was going to make it an early night! Classes start in the morning. Why in the world are they starting classes on a Friday?"

Gareth shrugged and smiled. "They're a queer lot, here. When is your first lecture?"

"At nine."

"Mine as well. I'll be seeing you at breakfast, then."

"Yes. Thanks for the coffee!"

I walked down the quiet hall and the staircase, out onto the dim starlit lane. Looking back, I saw an already shirtless Gareth leaning on his windowsill watching me.

"Nos da," I called softly.

He looked surprised and smiled. "Nos da!"

6 🌿

Ethan's Letter

"So, are we ready for classes, boyce?" Laney asked the table full of Americans at breakfast.

Everyone laughed. "Boyce"—the Welsh pronunciation of "boys"—was how the male Welsh students addressed a group, any group, even one made up of women!

"I guess so," said Karen Collier, shaking her long blonde hair and sighing. "I don't know, though. I've heard so many terrifying things about the British education system that I don't know what to expect!"

"Rob said it isn't much different from college in the States," I told her, and Jim Larrison nodded. "Remember, this isn't a school designed for people who have come up through the British system. At least, our part isn't. No use worrying about it before it happens, anyway."

Karen shrugged and said, "I guess not. What's your major, Jim?"

"Chemistry. What's yours?"

"Education." She turned to me. "What about you, Morfa?"

I swallowed my spoonful of Alpen cereal. "History. European. Laney, what's yours?" I asked, suddenly realizing that I had never talked with her about what she was studying.

"Welshmen," she answered emphatically, and everyone laughed again.

Conversation broke up into smaller groups, and I was concentrating on my cereal when Laney, sitting across from me, whispered sharply, "Psssst. Hey, Morfa. Look who's here."

I glanced over at the door. A somewhat sleepy and rumpled-looking Gareth yawned as he presented his meal ticket to the lady behind the counter. I wondered with a slight chill up my spine which Gareth he would be this morning: the usual austere one, or the friendly one of last night.

I didn't have to wait long to find out. He spotted me immediately and cut out of the food line to come straight over.

"Morfa, bore da."

"Bore da, Gareth," I answered, carefully pronouncing it BOR-ay DAH. Good morning.

He smiled approvingly. Laney watched with open interest and the other Americans fell gradually silent. I kicked Laney under the table, and she attacked her cereal zealously. But I knew she was still listening.

Gareth ignored all the other Americans. "I have lectures until supper, but I want to talk to you. Are you free after?"

I nodded. "Sure. I'll be up in my room." He had been up there with Arianwen and Rhys so I didn't need to tell him the room number. Realizing how this would look to the other Americans, I flushed.

He didn't notice. "Right, then. Your first lecture is Welsh, is it?"

"Right . . ."

"Lwc dda!"

This meant 'good luck,' I knew. "Diolch yn fawr."

The green eyes lit up and Gareth smiled. "You're very welcome." Then he turned and went back to the food line.

Refusing to look at any of the still-silent Americans, I stared outside as I drank my orange juice. But I could hardly keep on avoiding Laney's triumphantly grinning face indefinitely. "Oh Laney, shut up!" I finally said, laughing.

"I didn't say a word," she announced solemnly. "It wasn't necessary. Well, gang?" She turned and addressed the other Americans. "What do you think?"

Lisa Braddock looked at me and said, "I've been watching that guy ever since we got here, just hoping that I'd have a chance to get close to him! How did you do it?"

"I haven't done anything! He's a friend of my roommate's, that's all."

"Why does he want to talk to *you*, then?"

"I haven't the slightest idea. We talked about Welsh Nationalists last night . . . maybe it has to do with that."

"I wouldn't waste my time talking politics with *that* one." Karen smiled slyly.

Annoyed, I thought, maybe that's why it took him so long to be civil to me. He thought I was like you.

"I told Laney and I'm telling the rest of you, as far as I'm concerned he's open game," I said.

"I think, as far as *he's* concerned," said Laney, "the season's over."

"You're nuts," I answered rudely, then kicked her to apologize. "Come on, we're going to be late."

On the way up the steps from the canteen, we met Rhys coming down. "Laney, Morfa, bore da!" he said cheerfully.

"Bore da, Rhys."

"Rhys, baby, what's up? Have you seen Steff this morning?"

Rhys laughed. "I woke him this morning and then found

him asleep again in the shower! Kept him up past his bed-time, is it, Laney West?"

Laney laughed and shrugged. "I read in a science digest that people only really need an hour of sleep every night. I'm trying the theory out on Steff. Hey, where's the Welsh literature room, do you know?"

Rhys gave her directions, then turned to me. "What's your first lecture, Morfa fach?"

I smiled at the endearment. "Welsh. I think I'll skip it."

"After all my lessons, and Arianwen's? You'll amaze and frighten old Pritchard, I'm sure."

"Ha! Frighten, maybe. Well, if I'm going to do it, I'd better hurry or I'll be late."

"You'll do fine! Later, then." Rhys went on down the steps and Laney and I raced to the Academic Building.

The stern, gray-bearded professor's appearance fulfilled all of my fears and inspired new ones. Fortunately I wasn't late. A few students trickled in behind me. Jim McNae waved encouragingly to me from the back of the classroom as I took a seat, and somehow that helped a little.

When everyone was settled, Mr. Pritchard strode to the front of the classroom and tapped sharply on the desk with a long pointer.

"Well, then. Bore da, students. Who knows what that means?"

"Good morning," I said automatically, then jumped as he swiveled to stare at me. Oh no, I didn't raise my hand, I thought. I'll be expelled.

"Name?" he barked.

"Morfa Owen," I answered nervously.

He consulted a sheet of paper, then nodded shortly. " 'Good morning' is correct. Da iawn, very good. Students, repeat. Bore da."

"Bore da," the class repeated obediently. I sank a little lower in my seat with relief. So far, so good, I thought.

"So what do you think of the harp class?" Laney asked as we walked back toward Mair Hostel after supper.

"I like it, so far. Of course we didn't really do much today. Did you have anything else this afternoon?"

"No! Isn't that luxurious? Welsh Lit this morning and Harp after dinner, and then Steff and I spent the afternoon exploring. You had history, didn't you?"

"Yes, and guess who my lecturer is? Malcolm Davies!"

"You're kidding! Old 'tiny tots' himself?"

"The very same. He's as much fun in class as he is on tours. *And* he still calls us tiny tots!"

We laughed. I sniffed the cinnamon smell of roses and looked away at the hills. Beautiful . . . I hadn't done nearly as much exploring yet as I had planned to. It was wonderful to have a social life, but I wanted to take some time out soon and do some hiking. Maybe this weekend. "Can you believe that it's Friday night? Doesn't that feel silly, after only one day of classes?"

Laney nodded and laughed. "I don't know about these people! Though maybe they didn't want to shake us up too much all at once. Did you think classes were hard?"

"No, mine weren't bad at all. I had to pay attention, but really the hardest thing about them was paying attention to what my professors were *saying* instead of just sitting back and enjoying their accents!"

We passed by the large clump of trees separating college grounds from the field behind us. Suddenly I noticed that a ground fog was rising.

"Well! That came on suddenly, didn't it?"

Laney looked at me peculiarly. "What came on suddenly?"

I felt a sudden stab of fear. I looked quickly around again, and the fog was still there, much thicker near the trees.

From within the thick fog, between the trees, someone was watching me.

I stopped. It was the strange dark man from Glannant Road again, and this time there was no question as to whether he saw me or not. He stared at me intently, shook his head slightly. His eyes shone fierce and dark, but there was something anxious about them this time. As I stared, unable to move, he mouthed a word twice.

The word was, "Hurry."

My knees failed me suddenly and I crumpled to the ground.

"Morfa! What's the matter? Are you all right? Say something!"

I opened my eyes at the panic in Laney's voice. The back of my head was pounding furiously; I must have hit it when I fell. "I'm—I'm all right," I said shakily.

Laney slapped my face gently. "Did you hit your head? What made you fall?" She helped me to my feet.

"I don't know. I guess I hit my head. Did I—did I trip over something?"

We looked around on the ground, Laney seriously, I because I couldn't talk about what had really happened. I needed to think first. Besides, talking would make it too real. "I don't see anything, Morfa. Maybe it was something you ate. The food was even worse than usual tonight."

"Maybe that's it. Would you mind helping me back to my room? I'll be fine if I can lie down for a while."

Laney helped me into Mair Hostel and up to my room. As I lay down on the bed, she frowned and said, "Should I stay with you? I can go up and get some homework and—"

"Of course not! On a Friday night? Don't you and Steff have plans for a crawl?"

"Well, yes, but that isn't important—"

"Thanks anyway, chum, but I think sleep will do me more good than anything else. And I can do that just fine alone."

"If you're absolutely sure . . ."

Persuaded at last, Laney left, and I got up at once. My head still ached a little, but besides that I felt fine—physically, anyway. Mental and emotional states were a different matter.

Either the man existed, or I was going mad.

But if he did exist, why did no one else see him? Or the infernal fog he always seemed to bring with him? What did he mean by "Hurry"?

And how could he possibly be real, anyway? He couldn't just appear and start flitting in and out of my life and then disappear. It was impossible.

If I was not imagining it, he seemed to be trying to get a message across to me. Was it a warning—or a threat?

If I *was* going mad—

I actually jumped out of the chair when the knock sounded on the door. I waited, shaking, in silence. There it was again, loud and insistent. Everyone I knew was on crawl in town. *He* had followed us, seen Laney leave with Steff and come creeping up the stairs to the room where he knew I was alone.

There was a third knock. I realized that I couldn't keep away from him forever, and who knew how long he could lay siege outside the door? He seemed to know where I was and what I was doing anyway. Heart pounding violently, I strode to the door and threw it open.

It was Gareth.

I fell against the doorway in relief. Gareth stared at me,

concerned, and said, "Are you all right, then? I didn't mean to frighten you, but you said you'd be in your room after supper . . ."

"Oh, Gareth, I'm sorry. I forgot all about it. Laney and I—I saw a strange man watching us from the trees by the field after supper, and I was afraid that he had followed me up here."

"Be careful." Gareth frowned. "Sometimes there are old tramps around here. No one's been hurt yet, but take care anyway. Don't go out alone at night . . ."

"I won't," I assured him, and ushered him into the room. So that's what it is, I thought slowly, as he settled into the easy chair and I sat on the bed. I'm not imagining it, and I'm not going mad. It isn't any mysterious person, but just a tramp. I *had* better be careful! Wales didn't feel like the sort of place where things like that would happen. London, yes, but Wales?"

"Wales doesn't feel threatening at all," I said. "It feels like you ought to be able to wander around alone all night long in safety."

"The odds are you can, but why take chances?" asked Gareth.

"You're right, of course, and I won't. What did you want to talk to me about?"

Gareth leaned forward and clasped his hands around one knee. In ancient faded jeans and a light green shirt that glorified both the green eyes and the sandy flyaway hair, it was easy to see what Laney, Karen and Lisa were so attracted to. I felt a flush of pride that I could finally consider him a friend.

"You said last night that you liked the Arthur legends?"

I nodded.

"Well then, would you like to make a trip to Merlyn's Hill?"

"Merlyn's Hill! I didn't know there was such a thing! Where is it?"

Gareth got up and walked around to Arianwen's side of the room. I followed. He leaned down and pointed out her window into the distance.

"Right there. Three miles away, in Abergwili . . . we could walk it easy, if we began in the morning . . . But if you'd rather not, just say."

"Gareth, I'd love to! That sounds wonderful." I looked where he had pointed, and of course could see nothing as darkness had fallen. But I remembered seeing a tall hill from Arianwen's window when I first arrived. That must be it . . .

"Why do they call it Merlyn's Hill?"

"It's Bryn Myrddin, in Welsh, an' that's what it's usually called. Because he was supposed to have lived there. Didn't you know? Carmarthen . . . it's 'Caerfyrddin' in Welsh, 'Caer'—'fort,' and 'Myrddin'—'Merlyn.' Merlyn's Fort."

I was amazed. "I can't believe someone didn't tell me that before I came! My mam growing up around here and all . . . surely she knew."

"Maybe she wanted it to surprise you. Anyway, if you can get the backpack off your friend Laney, we'll pick up some food in town on the way."

"Great! When do you want to leave?"

Gareth pursed his lips. "How about half past nine? Is that too early?"

"No, that's fine. I'll be ready!"

He smiled and got up.

"Do you have to leave? Stay and I'll fix coffee if you like . . ."

He shook his head. "Sorry, but I promised some of the boys I'd go on a crawl with them . . . they're waiting at the gates. Thanks just the same . . . See you in the morning, then, is it?"

"Half past nine, at the gates."

"Right. Nos da."

"Nos da." I let him out and went to the window to watch him meet his friends at the gate. Merlyn's Hill and Merlyn's Fort! I hurried to my history of Carmarthen textbooks and looked through them to see what they had to say about Merlyn's connection with Carmarthen. When a bored Lisa Braddock showed up an hour or so later, we made coffee and talked about it. By the time I went to bed, I had forgotten the incident with the mysterious person completely.

"That's beautiful. What is it?"

Conversation had lagged but not uncomfortably, and Gareth had filled the gap by singing a beautiful slow Welsh song. "It's 'Pan Ddaw'r Dydd,' 'Until the Day.' By a Welsh singer, Geraint Jarman."

"It sounds very sad. Can you translate it for me?"

Gareth hesitated, then slowly translated:

"Walking down the street one moonlit night
And thinking of your face,
Rain falling on my head
And mingling with my tears,
Thinking about the dawn which is so far away . . .

When the day breaks,
Come into my life.

Lying, thinking, all alone:
Without you, how can I sleep?
Shaping poems in the murk,
But the imagery is anguished.

Oh, the color of your hair
And your tearful eyes!

Drinking coffee through each hour,
Watching news on TV;
Nobody calls here now.
It's hard to sleep,
Plagued by painful memories
Pain turns and turns . . .

When the day breaks,
Come into my life."

"It *is* sad," he added unnecessarily.

"It gives me chills," I said. "I love it, but how about something a bit more cheerful?"

Gareth smiled a quizzical little smile and launched into a happier-sounding song. I realized that every Welsh person I had heard singing had a nice voice. Was there such a thing as "tone deaf" in Wales?

We had met at the gates at 9:30 sharp and set off down Glannant Road. Saturday was market day in Carmarthen, and we pushed through crowds as we turned up Water and Lammas streets. After half an hour or so of walking, we circled around St. Peter's and I gave it a little bow when Gareth wasn't looking . . . Gareth pointed out the Roman amphitheater to me as we headed up the Lampeter Road.

We took the right-hand fork in the road, when it divided soon afterward, and headed for Abergwili. I kept lagging, pausing to soak in the view of the Towy River winding through the valley below us and the green bluffs overhanging it. The houses grew further and further apart, and I could tell we were nearing farming country. Gareth pointed out the old bishop's palace when we passed it, and then we came to, of all things, the Carmarthen Museum!

"What is the Carmarthen Museum doing in Abergwili?" I asked Gareth, startled and amused.

He shrugged. "Don't know. Remember, I'm not from Carmarthen, I'm from Swansea. I'm almost as much a stranger here as you! But look—"

He pointed up the road on the left-hand side. "That's Bryn Myrddin."

The hill was very tall and almost pointed. We would have to cross the road and take a small winding path to its base before we could start climbing.

Looking carefully for cars, we ran across the road, backpack bumping behind Gareth. Then we began to trudge up the hill path. More like a small road, really, I thought; big enough for one small car to drive on, though it would be a tight squeeze.

No sooner had that thought flitted through my mind than a sudden roar alerted us to a car coming around the bend ahead. "Get back!" Gareth shouted, and pushed me and himself flat against the embankment. Just in time. A small red Marina sped past, whooshing around the corner and squealing by inches from our feet. My eyes followed it and I glimpsed the letters "UTH" on the license plate. Uther Pendragon, I thought instantly; then, what a ridiculous thing to come to mind when we've almost been killed.

"Bloody idiot!" barked Gareth. "Good way to put us or him or both in the graveyard. Are you all right?"

"Fine. A little shaken up. Are you?"

He nodded. We brushed ourselves off and went on up the road, more cautiously this time. The path widened and hedges replaced the embankments on both sides. Just over

the top of the right-hand hedge, I could see the tip of
Bryn Myrddin.

"Hey, we're circling around the base of the hill," I called
to Gareth.

"I know. There should be a break in the hedge somewhere ahead where we can slip through and cut upwards."

"Gareth?"

He stopped and turned around. "What?"

"Nothing. Sorry. Let's go."

He shrugged, turned and went on. I followed, almost
reluctantly. I wanted to tell him that I was beginning to
get a very strange feeling about this hill, and that I wasn't
sure we should go on. But we had come a long way . . .
and it was stupid of me, anyway. Two, three hours of
walking wasted just because a breeze had come up and it
smelled threatening! I tried to ignore the feeling as well
as I could.

"Aha!" Gareth cried triumphantly. "A break!"

We stood at the entrance to it. It was a lane leading to a
farmhouse that looked as if it had been disused for a long
time. Paint peeled from the once white house, a part of
the roof had fallen in, and grass and weeds grew as high
as our waists clear up to the door. Only the lane appeared
to be usable.

"Let's just walk in a little and see where the top of the
hill is from here," said Gareth, and went through the gap
before I could stop him or tell him that as we entered the
drive, a wave of emotion had hit me so hard that I felt
nauseated. It was that smell . . . but it wasn't quite a
smell, somehow. I felt threatened and watched, but I also
felt fear and some terrible grief.

Halfway along the lane, Gareth stopped as if he had
run into a wall. I took a few steps toward him, feeling

more and more as if I were fighting some sort of current.
The threat and the grief became so intense that I shut my
eyes against it, unable to bear the feeling. My mind wandered to childhood memories: of classical music my father
had played, some of it anguished enough to confuse and
deeply disturb me; of my favorite stuffed animal which I
once left out in the rain; of the day my old dog had died . . .
but it was none of these things troubling me now. It was
the feeling that I was trespassing on someone else's emotions. Gareth's? No. These were the emotions of someone
who had experienced infinitely more than Gareth had yet.

Shuddering, I forced my eyes open and lurched toward
Gareth. Reaching him at last, I grabbed his arm as if it
were a lifeline. "Gareth," I gasped, and he slowly turned
anguish-filled eyes toward me.

"I feel," he said slowly, the usually smooth, accented
voice croaking, "as if everyone I cared for is dead."

"I know. Gareth, come on, we've got to get out of here.
Something's really wrong," and I began to pull him back
along the lane. He moved slowly, lurching as I had done,
both of us leaning heavily on one another. As we went on,
the feeling lessened, and the breeze with its strange smell
died down. But looking back, I thought I saw the whitish
blur of a face passing inside one of the farmhouse windows.

On the road, the air was still and the feeling had gone.

I leaned against the hedge, exhausted. Around us birds
chirped brightly and somewhere far away a cow was
lowing. Gareth looked at me silently, shaking his head.

"What was *that*?"

I laughed shakily. "I'm sure I don't have the slightest
idea! I think it almost killed me, though."

"If the car won't get you, the deserted farmhouse will,"
Gareth intoned absently. "Do you want to go on, Morfa?"

I looked back at the farmhouse, then at the old bent mailbox at the end of the hedge by my elbow. Pulling weeds back from the side toward me, I could see very faint, hand-drawn letters spelling the name of the house's long-absent owners.

Morgan.

I looked at my watch. It was almost one o'clock.

Sighing, I said, "Sure, why not? We've come so far, it would be a shame to turn back. But one more close call and we *will* call it quits, okay? Much more of this and I'm going to end up in a rest home."

Gareth smiled. "I'll be down the hall."

We went on up the road looking for another break in the hedge, and finally found one when we were just about to give up. It was very narrow and Gareth had to break off some small branches and push both sides of the hedge back before we could fit through. While he was doing that, I looked around and noticed all at once how quiet it was. The birds that had been singing earlier seemed to have flown away, and although we were surrounded by farms and farmland, no one was out at all. There weren't even any animals in the fields or the pens by the barns. How strange, I thought, for a Saturday afternoon! Or is it, I wondered, remembering that I still knew very little about Wales and its customs. Today was market day, after all; maybe everyone was in town.

Gareth pushed through the hedge at last and I went through afterwards. Ahead was a wide open field arching straight up Bryn Myrddin above us. Our goal was to top the hill and have our bread, cheese and wine in the woods on the other side. That was where Merlyn was supposed to have lived in his cave, which of course we would look for. Then we would head back to college and get there in time for supper.

It didn't seem as if we would have any more problems now.

When we started up the field, I heard what sounded like distant thunder. Gareth turned and looked at me inquiringly; evidently he heard it too. I shrugged and we ignored it, until we realized that it wasn't stopping. Instead, it was coming closer.

"Stop," said Gareth, putting a hand on my arm. We stood very still and listened. "That can't be thunder," I whispered, and he nodded. Whatever it was was coming from the other side of the hill. From the sound of it, it was coming *up* the hill.

Then, when it had become so loud that we covered our ears, it reached the top of the hill.

A gargantuan black horse wheeled and reared on the crest of Bryn Myrddin, tail and mane tossing. Its nostrils were dilated in fear or anger. It wasn't just the horse's being high above me that made it appear immense.

"Gareth." My voice shook. "Horses don't get that big."

He didn't answer but stared, transfixed. "Diawl," he whispered at last. "Diawl."

The horse shook its head, snorting furiously, and plunged down the hill directly at us.

Neither of us could move. I wanted to close my eyes, but I found I couldn't even do that. I stared, a lump rising in my throat as the huge black body hurtled down on us, closer and closer, flecks of froth flying from its mouth. It missed us by inches, wrenching us around with the force of its passing, and sailed over the hedge into the road behind us. Hoofbeats sped away in the direction from which we had come.

There was a long, breathless silence. Then I sat down abruptly. Gareth sat beside me.

"We'll go," he said at last, with a finality I wouldn't

have argued with even if I hadn't been glad to hear it. "But first," and he let the backpack drop from his shoulders, "I need a drink."

"Or twelve," I agreed.

Gareth flagged down Martin, the student-body president, who zoomed by in his little yellow car soon after we passed the bishop's palace. So we were saved the long walk back and arrived in time for a visit with Rhys and Arianwen, who were in our room, before supper.

Gareth seemed reluctant to tell them about the strange things that had happened to us on Bryn Myrddin, and the farmhouse driveway episode *was* rather difficult to believe in retrospect. But when I described the incident of the huge horse, Rhys looked so pointedly at Gareth, who so pointedly ignored him, that I impatiently said, "What?"

Speaking to Gareth, Rhys said, "Come on. You know what that was, don't you?"

"I know what you're thinking," Gareth answered reluctantly.

Rhys began to chant a Welsh poem quietly. Arianwen stood up and walked to the sink. Gareth looked extremely uncomfortable. "All right, enough," he said at last.

Arianwen turned the water on fiercely, and I jumped. She had a closed look on her face, as if she knew what they were talking about and wanted no part of it.

"What was it, Rhys?" I asked, ignoring but aware of Arianwen's angry glance and Gareth's forced boredom. "I've never seen a horse like that in my life."

"And you never will again. That horse belongs to no one. It was a witch-horse, one of the Horses of the Hills, which spend their lives running, running, and may never be stopped or caught. Other horses are terrified of them. I have always hoped to see one myself . . ."

"You know, even if you were right," said Gareth suddenly, cutting across my next question, "weren't these 'Horses of the Hills' supposed always to be white?"

Rhys shrugged. "You know the legend. But do you have another explanation for it? If there were a horse like that anywhere around here, everyone within fifty miles would know of it."

Gareth sighed and looked at his watch. Then he looked up at Rhys and grinned. "You're a batty old bugger, mun. Let's go to the canteen now, is it? It's mushy peas tonight; we don't want to be late for that!"

We all groaned and then laughed, tension easing.

The evening ended in a pub crawl. The black horse was not mentioned again, except in an aside to an incredulous Laney when we encountered her and Steff at the Guelder Rose.

But I returned to Bryn Myrddin that night in a dream and made it at last to the other side and Merlyn's cave. Merlyn presented me with a long silver sword which, he said, had been Arthur's.

"Morfa Owen," he said. "You have the same choice that Arthur had. And you will have to choose, when you come to the meeting place. Which will it be, little one?"

"I—I don't know what my choices are," I stammered.

"Come." And he led me to the mouth of his cave, where the trees and bracken I had labored through to reach it had vanished, and there was nothing but clear twilight sky. He raised a hand, and far in the distance huge gray clouds began to roll toward us. Soon the sky was filled with them, lightning flashing between them, deep thunder rolling.

"There is your choice, Morfa." Merlyn made a sweeping gesture with one hand toward the broiling sky, and with the other he gently touched the tip of the silver sword I held awkwardly and carefully. "There is your choice. The

Sword or the Darkness. Arthur chose the Sword, the bright shining Sword, and he died. But the failure was not in choosing the Sword, Morfa. It was in *Arthur's* choosing the Sword. It was the wrong choice—for Arthur. And now it comes again. Which is the right choice for Morfa? Can you wield the Sword? Can you call the Darkness down?"

I stared at the sword. "But Darkness is evil," I said haltingly.

Merlyn threw back his head and laughed. "Ah, Morfa! So much still to learn. Do not wait, child. Do not wait too long. One choice will exalt. One will destroy. When you reach the meeting place, it will be too late to choose. Either the sword or the Darkness must be in your hands. If your hands are empty, there will be no saving you."

I was wakened by something light dropping onto my face. I batted it off sleepily, then opened my eyes as Arianwen laughed.

"Here," she said, picking up a piece of paper from the floor. "You got a letter yesterday, but I forgot to give it to you."

I looked at the thin envelope with red and blue striped edges. The handwriting was Ethan's.

"I'm off," Arianwen said, opening the door. "Church calls. I'll see you at dinner, if you decide not to sleep all day!"

"Okay—bye," I said absently, and the door clicked shut. Sighing, I threw back the covers and slid out of bed. Toothbrushing, dressing and washing came before the letter, and as I sat down in the desk chair I chose an apple from the row on the windowsill. Breakfast wasn't served on Sunday mornings.

I nearly choked on my first bite as I read Ethan's opening sentence.

Dear Morfa,

I have reason to believe that our Morgan grandparents may still be alive."

I gasped and slammed the page down. Alive! That just wasn't possible. I had grown up knowing two things for sure about my mother's parents: that they had been Welsh and that they were dead. Alive! Then Mam had lied about them . . .

Well, she never actually told us that they were dead. The only one who used the word "dead" was Dad. Maybe he hadn't known any more about it than we had! But she never said they were *alive,* or contradicted him when he said they weren't. She must have known we thought they were dead.

What could be so terrible about them that she would prefer we think them dead?

I turned the letter back over.

I have reason to believe that our Morgan grandparents may still be alive. Don't think that you're the only one who's shocked! In fact, we aren't the only two. It was Sam, of all people, who found out about this.

You know his room is the closest to Mam's and Dad's. Well, it seems that he wasn't sleeping too well the night before last, so he sat up under the covers working on a new song by flashlight, so the light wouldn't disturb Mam and Dad. He said that at about one in the morning he heard a choked sort of cry from their room, and then Mam began to sob. All the time she was crying she was talking in a strange language. Sam said it sounded as if she were either pleading with someone or swearing at them! A strange combination, but that's what he said. There's your second shock of this letter: yes, Mam *is* a

Welsh speaker! He said pretty soon after this started, he could hear Dad asking what was wrong over and over and her putting him off. So then, bless his unethical little heart, he shut off the flashlight and crept out of bed into the hall outside their door so he could hear better.

When she finally stopped crying, she told Dad, "I've done something horrible, so horrible," over and over. Sam said it was really frightening. Dad kept asking her what it was and when she wouldn't answer, he started asking what language she had been speaking. Sam said she snapped, "Welsh, of course," and when he asked why she had never spoken it before she began to cry again. Finally she told him that she had had a dream about you in Wales, and when he cut in and told her not to let a dream upset her, she got angry and told him that the Welsh are true dreamers which he of course wouldn't know anything about, being half English. Sam said she made the word "English" sound like "leper." Then she said that her dream had been that you had found her mother.

Dad asked what was so terrible about your finding Gran Morgan's grave, and she said that was what was so horrible, that there was no grave to find. There was a long silence, except for Mam's crying, and then Dad asked in a low voice, "Do you mean that your parents weren't dead when you left Wales?" Sam said that she answered too low for him to hear, but that they were silent again afterwards so the answer must have been yes.

Finally Dad started asking all kinds of questions, as you can imagine, about why she and Aunt Angharad had left Wales and why she hasn't been in touch with her parents if they aren't dead. Now comes the really infuriating part. Mam ran out of the bedroom into the kitchen, Dad right behind her. They didn't see Sam, thank goodness, but though he crept up as close as he could to the kitchen, all he could hear were mumblings and crying until he finally gave up and went to bed.

So, kiddo, Sam called me today and told me about this. I've thought about it a lot and decided to go home as soon as I can and talk to Dad, and Mam too, I hope. Unfortunately I can't get away until Halloween weekend. But as soon as I know anything more, I'll let you know.

Halloween weekend. Halloween was three weeks away. I skimmed down the rest of the letter, which sketched Ethan's activities in college so boringly that I knew he was preoccupied with the main subject as I was. He returned to it in his final paragraph.

I don't know why thinking you might run into Gran Morgan would upset Mam so much and trigger all of this. Or why, if the thought horrifies her so much now, she didn't think of it before you left and stop you from going. But if I were you, I'd scour Trevaughan for some sign of the Morgans, if you haven't already. This is getting too strange . . . I feel as if the person we always thought of as Mam never really existed at all. She seems like a stranger . . .

I folded the letter slowly and slid it back into the envelope. Mam! Who are you, anyway? Ethan was right. My mental image of "Mam" or "Mrs. Owen" was becoming a totally imcompatible one with my new, vague image of "Gwenfair Morgan." Did she really speak Welsh? Why had she denied it—and she *did* deny it! And she had snapped at Dad about disbelieving her dream, calling him half English. It sounded just like what a member of

Gareth's Language Society, a Nationalist, would do. Was Mam a Welsh *Nationalist?* Then why had she left Wales? Who were these frightening grandparents . . . and if they were still alive, did they have the answers, and would they be more willing than Mam to give them?

Five minutes later I jerked open my door, jacket in hand, and almost bumped into Laney. She took a long look at my face and then said, "I was wondering when you'd get around to looking for your grandparents. Wait a minute and I'll get my jacket."

A minute or two later we scrambled up the embankment on the far side of Glannant Road and strode off through the fields toward Trevaughan.

7

Halloween

For the next three weeks, I searched for my grandparents, growing more and more discouraged as time went by. There was no "Ynyr Morgan" in the phone book, in any of Trevaughan's church registers, on a gravestone in either of its cemeteries. I asked about him at the Saturday market, at the public library, at the police station, at the town hall, with no success. "Ynyr," I found, was not as common as Dai, but not as uncommon as Manawyddan either. There was an Ynyr Jones in Trevaughan, and a schoolboy Ynyr Gwilliam, but no Ynyr Morgan. Laney went on crawls with me in Trevaughan pubs, where I would drop a mention of a local tragedy involving an Ynyr Morgan about twenty-five years ago, but while some of the locals were interested and said yes, that rang a faint bell, most shook their heads firmly and said no, they had lived here all their lives and there had been no such tragedy. My heart leaped when an old man set down his Double Dragon and, rubbing his stubbly chin, said, "Ynyr Morgan, is it? Wasn't he the bloke years ago with the beautiful twin daughters?" But the others shrugged and sipped, and he said he couldn't remember any more. I left the pub heavy-hearted, not knowing where else to turn. Laney stalked along silently beside me, deep in thought.

If it hadn't been for my grandparents, life would have been glorious for me those three weeks. Lectures were interesting and fun. I labored away on a short story about Nationalism for Creative Writing, about which Gareth, Rhys and Arianwen, who were Nationalists, Steff, who spoke Welsh but was not a Nationalist, Laney and I had some exciting discussions. I had advanced to a two-handed Welsh folk tune on the harp and was at the top of my Welsh class thanks to Rhys, who persisted with my Welsh tutoring. I had chosen the theme of Roman rule in Wales for my Celts term paper. Carmarthen and the Surrounding Communities was the highlight of my academic life, due to Malcolm Davies of "tiny tots" fame. The class spent most of its time in town studying the architecture from different periods of history, examining the street gratings and finding out what can be learned from them, visiting the town hall and its records vaults for more insights into local history. I was the only American in the class, the lectures were given in Welsh, and I was very proud when I could keep up and even occasionally answer in Welsh when Dr. Davies asked me questions.

Evenings were spent studying, going to parties or dances and on crawls in town. There were a lot of costume dances in the Union, called "Fancy-Dress Balls," with silly themes like "Vicars and Schoolgirls," when one could go dressed as either one or a combination of both! And movies were shown in the Union some nights. Often Arianwen and I would take a break from studying at eight or eight-thirty to dash to the Union shop and buy a package of chocolate biscuits . . . then end up staying much longer than we had planned, because Laney was there putting five of our favorite songs on the jukebox, or Rhys and Gareth were playing pool, or Steff was buying a round at the bar. Live bands played on weekend nights at the Union, and these were the best affairs of all. Everyone danced until one or two in the morning, then wandered in groups and couples back to the hostels for post-dance parties or quiet rendezvous.

Because Gareth and I ended up together after almost all of these occasions, Laney decided that we were having a passionate affair. We were having nothing of the kind. But since Laney and Steff and Rhys and Arianwen *were* very involved with each other, that didn't give us much choice but to end the evenings alone. Usually we talked about Nationalism. "Wales for the Welsh, and all the Welsh Welsh-speaking" was the code that Gareth lived and breathed by, and I sympathized deeply, though I didn't think there was really much hope of its ever coming true. I thought of Laney telling me weeks ago that she wouldn't want to date a Nationalist because his mind would be on politics instead of on her, and I knew by now that she was right. Gareth didn't date anyone, which was highly unusual for a Welshman unless he was a hard-core Nationalist. Why should they? Commitment to a woman meant responsibility and sharing decisions and having to make time for someone else. Commitment to the Nationalist cause could mean late-night raids on radio stations, perhaps even bombings of English homes in Wales, being jailed, and possibly martyrdom! These were excitements that did not go well with marriage.

I knew that Gareth's interest in me was dependent on my interest in Nationalism. As I was interested in it, with or without Gareth, we got along beautifully.

As autumn drew to a close and winter approached, there were many more rainy days. Unlike most of the other Americans, Laney and I loved the Welsh rain. It fell steadily but so lightly that I never bothered with an umbrella. I had bought an Army surplus raincoat before leaving the States, a wonderful ankle-length, drab green one that kept me very snug. And the rain kept everything around us a fresh, bright green. In the field that we splished through on our way to the secret grotto, the grass was as long and lush as ever.

There wasn't much chance to think about Mam a lot during the daytime, but sometimes at night, when I sat alone at my desk and thought I was studying, I would suddenly realize that I was thinking about her instead. And often I woke in the middle of the night from a dream about Mam, losing the dream in the same moment. My heart skipped a beat one morning a few days after I had received Ethan's letter, when I went downstairs to check the mail and spotted an envelope addressed in Mam's handwriting. But it was just a chatty, newsy letter, with no mention of my grandparents at all and no hint of anything wrong. Suddenly furious, I hurled it into the trash. There was no further word from Ethan.

The Friday before Halloween, Arianwen and I decided to go on a crawl in town. We hadn't visited the Ceff in quite a while, and we wanted to go to the Guelder Rose and Jackson's, which had the best jukebox in Carmarthen. We discussed our plan with Rhys, Gareth, Steff and Laney. Rhys and I decided to go into town early and eat, as we had missed supper in the canteen because of our exams. Laney wanted to practice the harp, Arianwen's parents were going to phone her at seven thirty, and Steff and Gareth had a soccer club meeting at seven. So we agreed to meet at Jackson's to start the crawl at eight sharp.

Rhys and I boarded the bus in front of Carmarthen College's curving entrance gates about six thirty. It was unusually crowded for this time of night, which was normally slow. Rhys and I made our way down the aisle to the one empty seat near the center, lurching as the bus roared off again and, even when we were seated, hanging on to keep from falling sideways when the bus made its hairpin turns. I could see the driver's face in the mirror above his seat. How could he drive the way he did and look so impassive, almost as though he were doing it in his sleep? The stone wall rose on either side of us. I glanced around at the other passengers, then froze as the feeling that someone was staring at me from behind seized me.

Ever so slowly, I turned away from Rhys sitting on my left and glanced around nonchalantly at the person behind me. But then I forgot to be nonchalant.

Dark hair brushing the top of a dark collar on a dark cloak, brilliant blue eyes clouded this time with what appeared to be—tears? The dark man nodded slowly, sadly, at what, I had no idea, and then lifted a hand from his black-cloaked lap and reached for me . . . to strangle me? To shake hands? To point something out? I didn't know, and all I could do was watch that rough brown hand draw closer.

The bus ground to a halt, and Rhys was up and urging me down the aisle and off the bus before I could speak or protest. We stood still as the bus careened away, and the shock must have been evident in my eyes because Rhys grabbed me firmly by both arms, gave me a shake and said, "Morfa, what is wrong?"

"Nothing," I said automatically, instantly regretting it. I didn't know what was going on or what to do, and if anyone would take me seriously and try to help it would be the mystical, sensitive Rhys.

"No, Rhys, it *isn't* nothing at all," I added quickly. "But it's a long story. Can we get some food and then talk? I'm shaken up and nervous and terribly hungry."

"Wrth gwrs, fach," he said comfortingly, patting me on the shoulders. We walked down the dark street past the teeming Ceff until we reached the Chinese take-away restaurant, one of two eating places in town that stayed open past five-thirty and wasn't a bar.

"I'll go in and order then, is it? You stay out here. It'll be hot and smoky inside."

"Thanks, I will," and as he went through the door and it swung shut behind him, I settled onto the window ledge under a streetlight to wait.

Although crowds were visible through the pub windows all around me, there was almost no one on the streets. A cool breeze blew, and the stars were spread magnificently across the sky. The moon was nearly full, I noticed, and smiled. It would be full the next night for Halloween festivities at Llansteffan Castle.

Far away, in the direction of the Guelder Rose, there was a sudden snatch of laughter and music as someone opened the door, then closed it again. A lone car drove up the street, circled the roundabout and cruised off toward Lampeter. I sighed and put my hand on the stones in the window ledge. They were cold and gave no comfort.

I jumped as someone touched my arm.

"Sorry!" Rhys laughed and handed me a paper bag of steaming hot food. "I forgot to ask what you wanted! So I got your usual, mushroom omelette and chips . . ."

"That's fine," I reassured him. We walked up Heol Dwr, Water Street, until we reached Lammas Street and its benches. No one was around. We sat down and opened our bags of food.

"Now," said Rhys. "Tell me what has been upsetting you."

So I told him everything. I began with the fog on

Glannant Road, then the return of the fog and the dark man's presence on college grounds, and finally the dark stranger behind me on the bus. And then I told him about my mother's secretiveness concerning her Welsh parents, my resolve to find their graves, Ethan's letter telling me that they might not be dead after all and my fruitless search for them in Trevaughan. Rhys listened silently, except for occasional soft exclamations of "Diawl" and "Duw."

When I finished, he took my hand. "Tell me, fach, why did you keep this to yourself for so long?"

"Oh, Rhys. Who would believe me?"

"I believe you."

"I know." I squeezed his hand appreciatively. "But I wasn't sure you would until the night Gareth and I came back from Bryn Myrddin."

"I don't understand—"

"The Horse of the Hills. You were amazed, but you believed us immediately. Arianwen didn't. Laney, when I told her later, believed it—bless her, she would believe me if I said I had climbed to the moon—but it didn't really touch her. She knows about the mystery of my grandparents and has been wonderful, helping me with that. But this other business . . . she just isn't a mystical person. And even Gareth—" I sighed. "As time goes on the horse gets smaller and smaller in his memory, and as for the incident on the farmhouse lane, that has faded altogether. At least, if he still believes it happened, he won't admit it. And it *did* happen, Rhys! All of it really happened! But none of it seems to mean anything. I have the feeling that I'm supposed to be doing something, but I don't know what, and if all these things that are happening are supposed to be clues, they're just leading me around and around in circles!"

I stopped, close to tears of frustration. Rhys looked at his hands, then up at me. "Do you think all of this has to do with your grandparents?"

This startled me. "Why would it?"

"I'm not sure. But I'll tell you one thing, Morfa. If there was a tragedy in Trevaughan twenty-five years ago, most of the people you talked to there remember it."

I stared at Rhys. "What do you mean?"

"I mean that either your mother has lied to you and the 'tragedy' never occurred, or it *did* happen and the townies are keeping it quiet."

"Rhys! Why would they do that?"

He shrugged. "Could be it brought some shame on the village, or someone asked them not to talk about it . . . Or it could be something else."

I waited. "Well, *what* else?"

He began to count off occurrences on his fingers. "You come to Wales to search for your grandparents and what happens? First you fit in with Welsh students so well that we swallow all of your free time taking you about with us. This has never happened before with an American, Morfa. Not so fast. And none have learned the language as you have, so fast or so well. Then a wild car, a strange breeze and a fierce witch-horse keep you away from Bryn Myrddin. A strange man frightens you from going out alone at night. A village full of natural wag-tongues falls silent when you come round asking about—what? About what happened to your grandparents twenty-five years ago. Something is trying to keep a secret from you, Morfa, and I think it must concern your grandparents."

My head spun. "Why do you say 'something?' Who could arrange all this? How could anyone talk with every person in Trevaughan and tell them to keep quiet when I come around and also arrange for the car and the breeze and the horse? Come on, Rhys!"

"Impossible, yes, if we are talking about a person. I am not talking about a person."

I was silent. "You mean a—like, a force?"

Rhys leaned back on the bench. "I believe that when a person is very deeply involved in an emotion—fear, anger, tension, excitement—he becomes aware of other forces moving in and around him. In the air. In the river. In the trees. In the stones. In the earth itself. Forces that work independently of us, but which sometimes cross our paths."

I thought of St. Peter's.

"Perhaps the car on the Bryn Myrddin road frightened you enough that you were able to feel the anger and grief of one of those forces on the farmhouse lane . . . even Gareth felt it. Or maybe it was aimed at you, Morfa. There are people who can open doors and walk in worlds unknown to us. People who can tame the powers of Darkness and Light . . . no, 'tame' is not the right word. Use them. Channel them. Borrow some of their power for their own purposes, or release some of that power into our world to work its own strange will."

But I was barely listening now. "Powers of Darkness and Light" . . . Where had I heard that before? "Powers of Darkness . . ." and suddenly I remembered.

"Rhys, I had a dream." I told him about returning to Bryn Myrddin and being given Arthur's silver sword by Merlyn.

"He told me I had to choose between the Sword and the Darkness, and asked me if I could call the Darkness down, or something like that. I said that Darkness was evil, and he laughed at me."

"I'm not surprised! He was a worker for the Dark himself."

"Rhys, you can't convince me that Merlyn was evil!"

Rhys shook his head violently. "Listen, Morfa. Dark was

not evil until what it represented became a threat to the ruling class. When the Roman armies came to Britain, to Wales, what did they find? You're studying it for your Celts class. What people were here?"

"I'm not sure what you—"

"Were they warlike? Were they savages?"

"Of course not! They were very civilized, more so than the Romans, I think. They were peaceable and lived quietly in small groups, all coordinated by a network of what I guess you would call priests and priestesses, though they were much more than that—"

"They were called Druids. The fierce Druids, who placated pagan gods with sacrifices—"

"Oh, they did not! I've been studying it. It's a common misconception that the Romans started when they wanted to undermine the power of the Druids so they could take over Britain more easily. They were peaceable, and there is no evidence of any human sacrifices. They were scientists, musicians, astronomers, lawgivers, judges and builders, as well as priests and priestesses."

Rhys nodded his head, smiling, and I realized that he had been testing me. "Yet their gods are the ones referred to as 'Dark,' Morfa, as well as their beliefs, their way of life, their civilization. And the Roman civilization is 'Light.' Which would you choose? If you could live in either system, which would it be?"

I hesitated only for a moment. "Theirs," I said. "The Druids'. The Dark."

"And I as well. Dark was not evil then, and *neither was Light.*"

I was confused. "What do you mean?"

"In the Old Knowledge, Dark is the symbol of intuition, of all that can be known without education. It is the symbol of feelings, of emotions, of what you know deep down is true, though you have no way of proving it. Light is the symbol of learning, of reason, of the logically correct choice. Both can be bad, and both can be good. It depends on what is being done with them and who is doing it. You, for instance. I think you are mostly a Dark person. You are very in tune with emotions, your own and other peoples', and with nature and feelings . . . you act on intuition more often than on careful reasoning, don't you?"

I nodded. I did.

"Arianwen is mostly Light. If she wants to go on a pub crawl but has an exam the next day, she will stay home and study. You would go on the crawl and stay up late studying, even though you knew you'd be tired the next day, or you'd skip the studying altogether. I'm not explaining this very well . . ."

"No, you're doing fine! And what are you?"

He smiled. "What do you think?"

I didn't even hesitate. "Dark. Because of the mysticism and the poetry and legends . . . and you're sensitive to other people's needs and feelings even when most people wouldn't notice anything at all. I see what you mean, at least about how Dark and Light is with people. But, what did Merlyn mean when he asked me if I could call the Darkness down? He spoke of it as if it were a separate thing. What did he mean, about choosing between the Sword and Darkness?"

"Well," said Rhys, "it seems to me that the sword would be a symbol of physical weapons, which are a tool of Light, and the Darkness is the power that a Dark person can gather from the earth and the elements. I think he was saying that you have to decide which you're going to trust; your physical strength and solid, physical weapons, or your psychic, mystical strength, that comes from Darkness."

"But I don't have any psychic, mystical strength! I never

even thought about these things before I came here . . . at least not since I was a child."

"He wouldn't have suggested it if you couldn't do it. It's finding out how to do it."

I sighed. "Where could I do that? Are there witches around here who give classes?"

Rhys smiled. "Not that I know of, I don't think you need to become a witch."

I smiled back at him. "Oh? What is a witch, Rhys? It sounds to me as if a 'witch' is simply—"

"—someone who uses intuition and the mystical powers of the earth and of the elements, who knows how to call the Darkness down," he finished with me. "Some are good and some are bad," he added. We stared at each other for a few seconds, and both of us jumped as a voice down Heol Dwr shouted, "Rhys! Morfa! Hiya, boyce!"

It was Steff, hand in hand with Laney, Arianwen and Gareth following. "Is it eight o'clock?" Rhys asked increduously. I looked at my watch and said, "It's ten after."

"Duw! Are you all right to be with the others now?" he asked in a low voice.

"Yes, I'm fine, but we'll have to talk again later."

"Right. Hey, get off, it's empty," he said to Steff, who had come up and snatched his paper bag.

"Isn't. There's a chip still," said Steff triumphantly, wolfing it down.

"What, are you hungry again?" Laney cuffed him on the shoulder. "Come on, you can get a bag of crisps at Jackson's."

" 'Tisn't crisps I'll be wanting at Jackson's," he said, wrinkling his nose.

"Yes, well, they have plenty of that, too. Come on," and Laney put her arm through mine and heaved me to my feet.

"Time for an after-dinner cider to settle the omelette grease. Hey, guess what? You had a caller while you were out. About half an hour after you left, wasn't it, Arian? Tell her."

"A caller! I don't know anybody here but all of you!"

"It was a phone call, not a visitor," Arianwen said. "Just after I talked with my folks. Your brother rang you up from America. Imagine! I spoke with him, and he's going to ring you again at about half past midnight. So we must be back by then."

Ethan calling from the States? He must have found something out! This *was* the weekend he had planned to go home and talk with Mam and Dad.

"Did he say what he wanted?"

She shook her head. "Na." She grinned slyly. "Sounded like a handsome bloke, though, is it?"

"I suppose he's fairly handsome," I said, smiling, while Laney laughed and said, "Did you hear that, Rhys? You have a rival!"

"Ah, well then, there we are," Rhys answered mildly.

"Morfa? I can barely hear you. How are you, kiddo?"

Ethan's voice was a bit fuzzy, but clear enough, and it unexpectedly made me homesick. "I'm great! How are you?"

"Just fine!"

"What are you calling here for, squirrel? It must cost a fortune!"

"It does! I wanted to know if you've discovered anything about Gran and Grandad Morgan. I didn't hear from you at all and I thought maybe . . ."

So he hadn't talked to Mam or Dad. I was bitterly disappointed. "No, Ethan, I've looked and looked everywhere and I can't find a trace of them. Dead or alive. One old man in Trevaughan remembered Grandad slightly, but didn't know anything about him that would help. Nobody else would talk at all."

"What do you mean, nobody would *talk*? That sounds deliberate! Do you think they know but aren't saying?"

"Maybe. I'm not sure yet. People remember things forever here, Ethan. Our grandparents must have moved away from Trevaughan ages ago. And if people don't want to talk—"

"Why don't they?"

"I don't know, but does it matter? If they don't want to I can't make them! All I know is that they definitely are not in Trevaughan, or buried in Trevaughan."

There was a short silence. "Is there any hope of tracing them?"

I had never known Ethan to be so dumb. "Tracing them from where? You have to have a starting point to trace someone! And all I have is a name that isn't even very unusual over here—"

"It isn't?"

"No! Unless something falls in my lap or you find out something else on your end, we're out of luck. Which reminds me . . . aren't you supposed to be at home this weekend slugging it out with Mam and Dad?"

"Yeah, well, I was supposed to be, but now I can't leave Columbia for another two weeks at least. I have to finish revising my honors thesis."

"Diawl!"

"What was that?"

"Nothing. Welsh. Are you sure?"

"Hey, you know I'd go if I could. I guess for the time being it's up to you, kid."

I bit my lip to keep from snapping at him. "Ethan, try

to get it through your head that there is nothing more I can do here!"

Awkwardly he changed the subject and talked for a few moments about his life in Columbia. I told him a few things about what I had been doing at Carmarthen College, and he assured me that all was well at home.

"My roommate says you sound cute," I told him.

"She does? Bring her home! I'm available, you know. Is she pretty?"

"Yes, but she's taken."

"Well, those are the breaks. Listen, kid, I've got to go. Sorry I didn't have more news for you."

"Likewise. Take care of yourself and write as soon as you get a chance to go home, all right?"

"Okay. Be good."

"You too."

"Good-bye, Morfa."

" 'Bye."

There was a click and I was alone.

I sat in the phone booth for a moment before getting up to return to my room.

It was all very discouraging.

I fended off Arianwen's curiosity by telling her that Ethan wanted me to bring her home and climbed into bed.

Morning dawned misty and cool. Realizing that there was nothing I could do about my grandparents, I decided to visit the small college library and see if I could learn anything about the powers of Light and Darkness. I told the librarian that I was doing a theme on witchcraft legends for a class, and after some discussion he led me through a locked cage into a dusty, dank back room full of shelves lined with moldering books.

My disbelief when I discovered that the books were in no

order at all left him completely untouched. With an airy, "There we are," he went off, leaving me to sort through the hundreds of volumes or not as I pleased. Sighing, I got a chair to climb up on and began searching on the highest shelf. I didn't bother to go back to the canteen for dinner.

By suppertime I was deep in a few helpful books I had uncovered, but I set them on one end of the table quickly when Arianwen came to fetch me. The librarian locked the cage door behind me and promised not to move the books or take out my page markers. Books in the cage couldn't be taken out, and, as I had found a book of spells in Welsh, I planned to try and translate them with my Welsh dictionary after lectures on Monday. The library, of course, was closed on Sunday.

It was Halloween, and I began to get excited despite myself when we walked down the lane to the canteen. Talk at supper was almost solely about the night's activities. First, there was to be a party and bonfire at Llansteffan Castle, a half-hour's bus ride away. Llansteffan Castle . . . atop a cliff that jutted out over the sea, high above a long, narrow beach with woods at either end. It was in ruins, but with enough left standing over a large area to remain impressive and foreboding, I was told. What better place to celebrate Halloween? After spending the evening there, busses would bring us back to the college for a fancy-dress ball at the Union. Tonight's theme, as mismatched as usual, was "Punks and Peers." "Peers?" I had asked Arianwen increduously when we first read the sign. How did one dress as a peer! "Lords and Ladies," she answered. Of course, in Britain "peers" meant peers of the realm, not members of one's peer group!

Neither Arianwen nor I ate much, and soon we were

hurrying back to Mair to put on old clothes for the castle party and complete our costumes for the ball. We had decided to go as ladies, dressing alike. Punks seemed more inviting, but we had few enough opportunities to look elegant. As Arianwen said, "This will make a change!"

Finally we were out in the lane, wearing jeans and "Carmarthen College" sweat shirts, in time to meet the bus. A small yellow car pulled up at the gates; it was Martin, with Gareth and Rhys, and Rhys stuck his head out a window to shout an invitation to Arianwen and me to ride down with them. She accepted, but I shouted back that I would ride the bus with Laney, thanks anyway, and off they zoomed. Laney showed up soon afterward and was glad I had stayed, because Steff had ridden down earlier with friends, too.

We sang as the bus bumped its way along the Llansteffan Road. Even Laney couldn't help but know the words in Welsh to the boisterous songs we heard around us every night in the pubs. It was cool, but the threat of rain had passed, and it looked like a perfect evening to spend at a castle beach. In between songs Laney and I chatted about classes and pub crawls and how our feelings about Wales had changed since our arrival, which seemed like six months ago.

The bus ground to a halt at a crossroads in the town of Llansteffan, and everyone piled out, pelting down the road that led to the beach. Within what seemed like minutes several bonfires had puffed and flickered into life up and down the beach. Firelit games of soccer were organized, and a group of Americans led by Jim Larrison and Karen Collier gave some of the Welsh students a crash course in baseball. The castle ruins loomed dreary and magnificent overhead. I was thrilled by them and would have stared indefinitely if Rhys hadn't grabbed me by the sleeve and forced me into the baseball game.

He proved to be the star, hitting the game-winning home run to his delight. The bonfires were roaring by this time, and it had grown quite dark. As soon as the last of the soccer games ended, everyone but the few elected to stay and keep the fires going began to climb up the cliff to the castle ruins. Rhys, Steff and Gareth stayed with the fires voluntarily, with a group of about ten more Welshmen. ("It's because," Laney whispered conspiratorially to Arianwen and me as we scrambled upward, "the ale is due to arrive any minute now. There won't be a drop left by the time we come back down!")

I was amazed at how vast the ruins proved to be. They were divided into two main sections by a low stone wall, with all sorts of little rooms and turrets to climb up into and high walls that would be wonderful to walk on, especially when—like tonight—there was no wind blowing. The sea was dark and beautiful below, and the moon glowed round over a far hill.

The big group semi-organized itself and we played a lot of games that were fun in a dark castle at night on Halloween. Mostly they consisted of hiding and scaring the wits out of whoever was unlucky enough to be finding! The group moved slowly from the sea end of the ruins to the land end. After the games died out, most of the Welsh students trickled back down to the beach. Most of the Americans sauntered around the ruins taking a more leisurely look.

Arianwen had gone back to the beach, and Laney walked slowly off across the grassy center of the castle arguing with Jim McNae about the conditions under which this castle had been destroyed. I was left alone at the sea end and decided, since there was no wind, to climb up on the outside wall and get a better look at the sea by moonlight. The stones were rough as I clawed my way up, but I made it to the top. The ocean stretched out calm and quiet as far as I could see into the distance. Just like Wales, I thought. Beautiful and dark . . . calm on the outside, teeming with activity under the surface . . .

I felt a sudden push on my spine and then I was falling.

Falling. I twisted as I fell and glimpsed a white blur of a face, grinning wickedly, before I twisted away again. There was nothing around me but the air I whistled through. I turned and turned, growing faint, feeling as if it was all in slow motion, a dream, expecting at any second to smack onto the ocean surface and plunge under, down, down, until I lost consciousness.

Instead I landed with a thud on thick, wet grass.

I lay very still, the breath knocked out of me. The castle ruins spun blurrily above me, the stars above them, spiraling faster and making me feel sick. After a geological age passed, they gradually came into focus. My head throbbed violently. My heart was pounding. But as I cautiously moved each arm and leg, I found that, miraculously, I wasn't seriously injured. And I realized just how miraculous it was when I heard the lap of water close by and turned my head.

I lay at the very edge of the ocean, and so close that my nose brushed them when my face was turned was a row of jagged rocks.

I pushed myself to a sitting position, swiveling to lean against the rocks that I might have been impaled on. I wasn't even very sore, I found, though I was sure I would be later. Only the thick, wet, matted turf between the woods and the water's edge had kept all the bones in my body from breaking. I covered my face, wanting to cry or be sick, but not having the strength for either.

And then I heard someone slipping and sliding down the cliff after me.

I couldn't look up. Whoever had pushed me saw that I was still alive, I thought, terrified, and was coming to finish me off.

"Morfa! My God, I can't believe you're all right!"

Waves of relief flooded over me. It was Laney.

She raced across the beach, dropped to her knees and hugged me fiercely. "I can't believe it! I saw you walking on the wall, turned to say something to Jim, then turned to look at you again—but you were gone! You couldn't have disappeared that quickly unless you had fallen over, and I was sure you had hit the rocks or gone underwater and drowned. How did it happen? Did you lose your balance?"

Chilled, I shook my head and said slowly, "You didn't see anyone else near where I had been?"

Laney shook her head. "No, why?"

"Laney, I didn't fall. I was pushed."

Laney gasped. "Pushed! But you couldn't have been! There was no one there at all! And they couldn't have run away that quickly, it wasn't two seconds after you fell that I looked again!"

"I felt a hand pushing me, and when I was falling I looked up and there was a face grinning at me."

"Did you recognize the face?"

I shook my head.

"Morfa, you must have imagined it. Maybe a wind came up so suddenly that it felt like a hand pushing you, and you were already sort of unconscious when you thought you saw someone. Because I swear to you, there was no one around! Who would want to hurt you, anyway?"

I almost laughed. But I realized that there was no point in arguing with Laney about it, so instead I gathered myself together and lurched to my feet.

Laney stood too. "Are you all right? Can you walk?"

I took a couple of steps and nodded. Laney looked back at the rocks I had been leaning against and turned to me, eyes wide. "Morfa Owen, I have never seen such a close call in my life."

I nodded, looking back myself. "I'll have to be more careful," I answered sincerely.

As we walked around the cliff to the other side, where the bonfires were, I said, "Laney, do me a big favor, will you?"

"Sure. What?"

"Does anyone but you know I—fell?"

Laney shook her head. "I didn't say a word to Jim, I just took off running and vaulted over the wall. He probably thinks he was just being unusually boring!"

"Good. Let's keep it that way, all right?"

"Morfa, you're kidding! Not even tell Gareth and Arianwen and Steff and Rhys?"

"No," and seeing Laney's disbelief I added, "Laney, think how embarrassing it is! My first time at Llansteffan and I go walking on the walls and fall off! Now would you want them to know if it was you?"

Laney thought a moment, then laughed. "I guess not."

"Of course not! Since I wasn't hurt, there's no reason for anyone to know . . ."

"No, I guess there isn't. Okay, mum's the word, chum. But if this ever happens again, I'm going to send an article about it *with pictures* to *News of the World!*"

"Hey, it *won't* happen again, I promise!"

Laney was quiet for a moment, then said, "You're still going to Punks and Peers tonight?"

"Why not? I don't think any of my dancing mechanism was broken! Halloween in Wales comes but once, you know."

"For you, it almost only came but once, period," Laney added.

"How do I look?" I asked Arianwen two hours later.

She inspected me and smiled. "I suspect Gareth's going to look past your politics tonight," she answered.

"I'll change, then," I said, but wondered what I would do if the handsome green-eyed Welshman *did* "look past my politics." It was too troubling a thought, so I concentrated on anticipating the dancing to come instead.

Arianwen and I were dressed in long white, shimmering gowns, with diamond earrings and necklaces, hair piled high on our heads and diamond tiaras. Of course, the gowns were really a combination of bed sheets, glitter from the local variety store and some clever needlework, and the diamond jewelry had come from Woolworth's, but it certainly looked like something from an upper-class London dressmaker's when the lights were dim! And the lights were always dim in the Union.

The Union was very dim indeed. We paid our twenty-five pence to Martin at the door. He whistled at us and said, "So *that's* the latest technique for not having to buy your own drinks!" We moved on into the main room and smiled at each other excitedly. A Welsh rock band with four members, called Y Llwyth (The Tribe), was already playing. The room filled quickly with punks and peers, dancing in the middle of the floor, lining up at the bar, ringing the room to watch the dancers and the band. Colored floodlights gave the dim room a festive air, and the pulsating beat was infectious. Laney swept down on us as soon as we arrived and started dancing, thrusting drinks into our hands.

"Here, these are on me!"

Arianwen laughed and said, "Martin said these costumes would get us free pints, but I didn't think he meant from you!"

Laney was the perfect punk in Steff's black leather jacket, tight jeans, Norwegian sailor's hat and an absurd chain-link necklace that clanked heavily against her collar bone as she danced.

"Doesn't that hurt?" I asked breathlessly.

"Are you kidding?" Laney laughed and waved her pint over her head, slopping it on the floor. "After a few of these, nothing hurts!"

Steff arrived, and he and Laney tangoed off across the Union toward the band. Then Rhys arrived, chatted with both of us briefly and boisterously and then whisked Arianwen off too. My pint glass was empty, so I went to the bar to refill it. On the way back to the dance floor I ran into Gareth.

I stopped and whistled. He wore a top hat, bow tie, white ruffled shirt under long black topcoat with tails and white dress gloves. His ever-present faded jeans and blue sneakers completed the costume!

He took my whistle in stride and extended his arm. "May I have this dance, Modom?"

I curtsied and made believe I was fanning myself shyly. "Thank you, kind sir; I believe there is a vacancy on my dance card, but I must consult my chaperone."

We laughed and made our way out onto the dance floor, where we spent most of the rest of the night. Whenever a stiff muscle reminded me of the event at the castle, I forced it from my mind as quickly as I could.

There was a loud, unanimous groan when the band

packed up at last and someone turned the overhead lights on. Gareth and I went outside and wandered around the campus grounds for a while, talking and laughing. Almost half of our conversation was in Welsh by this time, and I felt very close to him that night. When there was a long pause before he left me at the hostel door, I thought with a shock that he was going to kiss me. But he smiled at last, said a quiet, "Nos da," and, after I walked inside, turned and headed for Dewi. I surprised myself by feeling disappointed, but—after the horror of the fall at Llansteffan—the rest of the night had been wonderful, and I was cheerful again by the time I undressed and washed up. I was also wide awake, though it was close to 3:00 a.m., so I switched on the lamp and began a letter to Sheena.

I was slipping the letter into its envelope when I heard the doorknob turn and Arianwen entered the room. I turned, smiling, to ask how her night had been and why she was back so early—and dropped the letter.

Arianwen stood in the doorway, a pool of water collecting under her. Her sheet/dress was soaked clear through, and her hair was plastered to her face. Little bits of weed clung to the dress here and there, and there was a faint, unpleasant smell moving through the room. She must have been thrown into the stagnant pond beyond the Academic Building, I realized, horrified. Students were sometimes thrown in by their classmates for a lark, but *never* at night. The pond had cement edges, and it would be easy to misjudge a toss.

There was a long purple bruise running up Arianwen's left arm and a cut on her cheek.

"Arianwen, fach, what happened to you?" I cried, standing up in shock.

She paused, and I could tell she was fighting tears. "Rhys—Rhys left me outside the Union for a bit while he made sure it was locked up after everyone had left. I was looking over this way when suddenly someone grabbed me from behind. He held me so tight I couldn't turn around and see who it was. He carried me to the pond and threw me in . . ."

"But who would do something like that? Everybody likes you," I said, moving toward Arianwen to hug her. To my amazement, she drew back and stared at me with—hostility?

In a shaky voice, she said, "They didn't do it to *me*."

I let my arms drop. "What do you mean?"

She gulped down a sob. "Just before he threw me in—or she or whoever it was—he whispered in Welsh, 'We'll see if the pond can finish what the castle wall started, Morfa Owen'!"

My knees buckled and I barely managed to reach the desk chair again before collapsing.

"Oh, Arianwen. Oh, my God!"

8 ❦

The Cabbie

When Rhys came over half an hour later that night, assuming Arianwen had grown tired of waiting outside the Union, he had to be told about her. When Laney found out the next morning, she couldn't be kept quiet about the castle wall incident.

"It was one thing when I just thought it would embarrass you," she told me severely, "but this is something *else* again!"

"All right," I said resignedly, "I understand, and I'd do the same if it were you. Just don't let it get around among the other Americans, okay? It's more—oh, I don't know, it's just *different* with Arianwen and Rhys."

Whether she understood what I was trying to say or just felt sorry for me, she didn't tell anyone but our Welsh friends.

"This has gone far beyond reason, Morfa fach," Rhys said, shaking his dark head. Arianwen had gone into town for breakfast before he arrived and he was going to catch up with her. Since Jim McNae had called Laney out of my room to ask about their Welsh Lit assignment, he and I were alone for the moment. "The power is moving quickly and I cannot figure why."

"Perhaps because I've started researching the Dark?" I asked.

"Might be . . ." He sat on the corner of the desk and frowned deeply.

"Is the Light after me, Rhys?"

He looked up quickly and shook his head. "The Light and the Dark do not strive against each other, Morfa. When all is well, they work together in harmony. It is when the wrong power is wielded by the wrong hand that disharmony begins.

"And the forces are wild, fach. They are, like the earth, beyond human labels of good and evil. Is the earth good when the fields are full of grain? Is it bad when a drought leaves the land barren? No, wrth gwrs. But I am beginning to believe that the evil being done to you has human cunning behind it and human allies supporting it. And I don't know how to help you."

He looked out the window despairingly, and suddenly I was overwhelmed by how much this Welshman whom I had known for less than two months cared about what happened to me. I touched his shoulder and said, "Never mind, Rhys. It'll be okay somehow. If only I could get away from here for a while. Wouldn't it be nice," I said, trying to joke with him, "if I had some relatives close by? I could drop in on them for a few days, and . . ."

I let my voice trail off as he looked up at me swiftly, eyes lighting. "Morfa, perhaps that's it! Myn bran i, why didn't I think of that sooner? Ah, I'll have to check with Arian . . . Esgusoduch fi, fach?"

I excused him, and he hopped off the desk and raced out the door and down the stairs. Looking out the window, I saw him leave Mair and go running toward town.

What in the world was he up to?

"It's the perfect solution, Morfa, and you must go," said Arianwen in answer to my incredulous look.

Surely the harsh edge on her voice was only in my imagination.

Rhys, on the other hand, nearly rose from his seat in his eagerness. "Listen to her, Morfa! You don't have any important lectures on Thursday do you?"

I laughed. "Important" to whom? "No, not really. Laney can get the notes for 'Celts,' and the tutor already has told me that I can turn in my Creative Writing story early if I want to. But . . ."

"Magic! Then you'll come with me Thursday morning by rail to visit my family for the weekend in Cardiff."

"Rhys, what if they don't want an extra person to worry about all weekend? That wouldn't be surprising—" But he was shaking his head emphatically.

"I've rung them up already and asked," he said, grinning, "and they're anxious to meet you. There, now!"

"I don't want you to go home for the weekend just because I need to get away! I could take a train to the coast and stay in a bed-and-breakfast—"

"I told you, I was going home this weekend already! Mam wrote and said they wanted to see me . . . nothing special, but I haven't been since coll started. Don't you want to meet my family?" he added in an injured tone, obviously a new tactic.

"Of course I do," I said automatically, and then "All right, thanks. I'll be glad to come, and I'd love to look around Cardiff. Are you sure you can't come with us, Arianwen?"

She shook her head firmly. "Thanks, but I've exams to study for. It wouldn't get done if I were mucking about in Cardiff with you all!" She laughed and I smiled, while trying to figure her out.

"It's all settled, then," said Rhys happily, attacking his breakfast. I concentrated on mine also, trying to hide my amazement.

I was sure that Arianwen must be very angry. But that was hardly something I could discuss with either her or Rhys.

One thing I had observed to be a strict rule in Welsh relationships was that men and women could not just be friends the way Americans can. Oh, they could talk to one another, and a single person could go out with another couple, but if two members of the opposite sexes went to a film or to the pubs or to each other's rooms together, they were going steady. The only relationship like an American one that I had observed—one that involved a Welsh person —was my own with Gareth—and of course the only Welsh students who believed that it was a simple friendship were Rhys and Arianwen. I wasn't even sure about Arianwen. But one thing I did feel sure about in regard to her—she was not pleased that I would be spending a weekend alone in Cardiff with Rhys, her boyfriend. She didn't say so, but it was evident in her sharp-edged enthusiasm, in her quick, hard looks, in her too-bright smile. What must irk her most fiercely was that it was Rhys's idea, not mine, and it hadn't seemed to occur to him for a moment that it wasn't the correct thing to do. I had hesitated as long as I could in accepting Rhys's offer because I was afraid that if I did I would close the door on her friendship. But when it came down to offending either Rhys or Arianwen, I found that there was no doubt where my loyalties lay. Arianwen and I had been perfectly comfortable together as roommates, but we had never understood each other as Rhys and I did instinctively. It occurred to me that Rhys was far too bright not to realize his breach of conduct now toward Arianwen. About *why* he was doing it, I knew no more than she did.

Anyway, it was too late to worry about it. The decision was made, and I decided to concentrate on the fact that starting Thursday, I would have four whole days in which to forget about grandparents, strange violent powers and disappearing men.

Monday through Wednesday I divided my time between working on my Creative Writing short story and researching the Dark, as I had put it to Rhys, in the college and town libraries. "Calling the darkness down" sounded to me like invoking some sort of power, which meant a spell or chanting or something of the kind. So I concentrated most of all on translating the Welsh spells I had found in the college library book.

I don't think the book had been touched in years. Once very well used, to judge by the fraying edges and dog-eared pages, the spine crackled when I first opened it. I had to use incredible care to keep the pages from falling out. Some of the Welsh, I decided, must be archaic; it didn't sound at all familiar and my dictionary was no help in figuring it out. Because of conflicting class schedules, rugby games and the ridiculously early closing hours of the library, Rhys couldn't meet me there any of the three days to help me translate the spell I was pinning my hopes on. The title seemed to be something like "Raising Power," which sounded hopeful, but practically all I could make out was that it required five people. I mentioned it quietly to Rhys Wednesday night after supper, and he promised to come help me translate it as soon as we returned from Cardiff. I had considered asking Gareth but rejected the idea. He would ridicule the whole thing, I was sure. I didn't even consider Arianwen, who was now barely troubling to conceal her coolness toward me.

"You'll have to move up here with me, of course," said Laney, who had no roommate.

"Oh Laney! Thanks, but I don't know. Are you sure you want a roommate? You've always said you were glad to have a room to yourself . . ."

"What I said was that I was glad I didn't have a roommate."

"Well, isn't that the same thing?"

"No, because I meant a roommate that Rob chose for me. I was afraid that we might not get along. Or that something would happen like what has happened with you and Arianwen. But I've known you long enough now to know that we'd get along just fine. I think it would be a blast! But if you would rather stay where you are and slug it out, no hard feelings. I won't say, 'I understand,' because I wouldn't understand! But it wouldn't matter. Do what you want."

"I want to move in with you—thanks," I said sincerely, suddenly making up my mind. "But not until I get back from Cardiff."

"That should be a terrific trip, don't you think?" said Laney enthusiastically, tactfully switching the subject. "Do you two have any specific plans yet?"

"Well, he called his folks to let them know I was definitely coming, and he asked his younger brother to buy tickets to an International Rugby Match for us if he could. That sounds interesting, doesn't it? And I think we're going to visit the castle, and who knows what else . . ."

"Good. Just be sure you keep busy and don't waste any time thinking about classes or Arianwen or anything unpleasant like that."

"It may be a bit hard not to think about Arianwen," I said, getting up from Laney's bed and heading for the door. "After all, she and Rhys have been seeing each other for years. I imagine his family will remind me of her often enough."

This, however, was not the case.

Mr. and Mrs. Jones met Rhys and me at the station and were overwhelmingly kind to me. They hugged Rhys and asked him all kinds of questions about college, but never mentioned Arianwen. Back at the house, they settled me into the guest room, which Rhys told me used to be his married sister Rhiannon's bedroom, and informed me that I was free to retreat there whenever they got on my nerves. Not very likely, I thought! Younger brother Luc, who was my age, came skidding in just in time for supper. He squeezed my hand and presented me with two tickets to the rugby match between Wales and Rumania on Saturday. Rhys tried to pay him for them, but he was waved airily off. In Welsh, Luc told him, "You had the audacity to get to her first; the least I can do is buy her a rugby ticket!"

I laughed and said, "Diolch yn fawr—for the ticket *and* the compliment!" Luc turned scarlet, stared at me and then turned to Rhys accusingly. "She speaks Welsh! Why didn't you tell me?" Then he smiled and joined Rhys in delighted laughter.

Luc looked a great deal like Rhys, though he was fair-haired and beardless. Mr. Jones looked like a rugby player, too, but Mrs. Jones was tiny and delicate-looking, with the boys' arresting blue eyes and deep auburn hair. As we washed dishes after supper, I told her how healthy and strong I thought her family looked, and she smiled.

"Moving water does not stagnate, is it? Luc is still at home but not for long. When the boys were about fourteen and sixteen I began looking for other interests. It is not the number of years passing but empty time that makes one old."

Rhiannon, the married sister, came over that night with her husband, a professor of Welsh at the University in Cardiff, and their small blonde daughter. I spent a quiet evening playing with the little girl, Bethan, reviving games that I had played with my own sister Megan when she was small. The family spoke mostly in Welsh around a comfortable fire in the fireplace, and I understood enough to join in now and then. I was happy that they were relaxed enough around me not to interrupt their enjoyable routine.

I loved Cardiff. Rhys and I rode everywhere on double-decker buses: to the castle, to the market, into town to pick up some things for Mrs. Jones. We ate curry at an Indian restaurant and walked along the docks chatting with short, burly sailors. At night, Luc joined us and we danced in hot, electric nightclubs with good Welsh bands and flashing lights. Between sets we drank cider and ale and had the usual shouted and amiable arguments with locals about everything from the weather to the inevitable politics.

Saturday afternoon was the rugby match against Rumania. Rhys and I left early. I was wearing the red and white striped scarf that Mr. and Mrs. Jones had given me. "It's Wales's colors, now. It'll bring you luck!" Mrs. Jones had said, waving off my astonished thanks.

The bus ride was long and bumpy, and the streets were packed with Welsh rugby fans celebrating in advance. Red and white banners fluttered from windows here and there as we approached the stadium. It was all very exciting.

I squeezed Rhys's arm. "This is wonderful!"

He laughed at me and squinted up at the sky. "I just hope it doesn't rain! Looks as if it might."

We pushed our way through the crowds at the gate, fans crowded around vendors selling food and souvenirs.

"Sorry, no cider in the stadium!" Rhys grinned.

"You're kidding—what a horrid place!"

We climbed up to our seats, and soon afterward the game began. I was fairly well acquainted with the rules of rugby by this time, having watched Rhys play, and he filled me in on what I didn't understand. The only surprise was provided by the fans, and belatedly I remembered Aunt Angharad telling me that Welsh rugby crowds sing songs to encourage their players! It was impressive, those thousands of harmonizing voices. Everyone stood for the Welsh national anthem at the beginning of the game, and as always, I was deeply moved by how seriously everyone treated it. At home, the only place I ever heard our anthem was at baseball games when about a tenth of the crowd bothered to sing at all. But of course here, the anthem and the language were about all the independence these people had. No wonder they treated the anthem so reverently.

I was familiar with the song by this time and sang it in Welsh with everyone else.

> "Mae hen wlad fy nhadau yn annwyl i mi,
> Gwlad beirdd a chantorion, enwogion o fri,
> Ei gwrol ryfelwyr, gwlatgarwyr tra mad,
> Tros ryddid collasant eu gwaed.
>
>> Gwlad! Gwlad!
>> Pleidiol wyf i'r gwlad.
>> Tra mor yn fur ir bur hoff bau,
>> O bydded i'r hen iaith barhau."

> "The land of my fathers is dear to me,
> Land of bards and singers, famous men of renown,

Its brave warriors, such good patriots,
For freedom they lost their blood.

    Land! Land!
    I am faithful to my land.
    While the sea is a wall to the pure, dear country,
    O let the old language continue."

"Land of my fathers?" I thought as I sat down and a deafening cheer rose around me. "Dad has nothing to do with it where I'm concerned, anyhow. It should be "Land of my mothers." There was much that I couldn't understand about my mother, but one thing I was beginning to understand was why, after twenty-five years, she still missed Wales as if it were her first day away. In spite of everything that had happened to me, I couldn't bear to think of leaving, either. Because life had a power, here. Perhaps the Dark and Light that Rhys talked about was closer to the surface in Wales. I wasn't sure, but I knew that beneath the probably useless political struggles of the Welsh and deeper even than the worthwhile fight to preserve the language and heritage of Wales, there was a fierce, primal *urgency* to life here. It was like whatever had driven people of all eras to build places of worship on the site of the Carmarthen stone circle at St. Peter's. On quiet nights out in the fields around the college, if I was very still, I could feel a heart beating in the hills, the earth's blood rushing through the veins of the rivers, I could hear a rhythmic, living breath rush through the treetops. It seemed to fill me with a thunderous, overwhelming need to create, to learn and to rejoice. Something seemed to whisper, day and night, waking and sleeping, to me: live, as I am living, with heart and body and spirit, because every moment of your life is important, every move you make a step in the great cosmic dance. That was it—a sense of *purpose*. We don't have it in the States, I thought, or we've lost it . . . yes, we've lost it, I decided, remembering how closely tied the Indians were to the land. We've smothered it, that's why everything seems so much more mundane and purposeless at home; that's why you have to work hard to motivate yourself. Too much cellophane and styrofoam and concrete. Too many offices and cars and shopping centers. Who even looks at the land nowadays—except as a curiosity on Sunday drives? There are so few people at home who still respect the land, who still interact with it every day. But here they still respect the land, and the land exerts its power. Not a good or an evil power; it's not as simple and black-and-white as that. But an ancient, aware power with a wild earth-wisdom and some strange earth-purpose. Dark; yes, it's Dark. And I belong in that power.

Another wild cheer shocked me out of what had almost been a trance. "What happened?" I asked Rhys, who had jumped to his feet.

"A try!" he shouted happily. "Wales is winning!"

"Did you enjoy the match?" Rhys asked as we moved slowly down the stadium aisle.

"Oh, yes! I'm glad Wales won." The Welsh team had beaten Rumania 13-12, and those who hadn't already drunk themselves almost into blissful unconsciousness were leaving immediately to do so. The crowd seemed to jam at one of the gates, and the mob became a crush.

Then a fight broke out.

People were so closely packed that the entire crowd surged and swayed as the fighters knocked into more and more people. Many of them began to slug back furiously.

We were held immobile in the mob, Rhys holding me tightly while my heart thundered, until finally we heard distant sirens approaching and a great crash as one of the stadium gates went down under the pressure. The crowd plunged through the opening, with such sudden force that I was jerked away from Rhys and pulled forward so quickly that in a moment I had lost sight of him. I found myself halfway up the block before I could twist around and try to find him.

"Rhys! Rhys!"

It was ridiculous to shout; I could barely hear myself. The crowd moved like a wave up the narrow side street, turning this way and that, until finally it began to slow, calm down and sort itself out. At last I was left panting and battered on a cobbled street in the middle of town. I was totally lost.

After a moment of panic, I wasn't too badly frightened. Cardiff was big but not *that* big, and I knew I could find some place where I could get my bearings before long. Then, if I found I was too far from Rhys's house to walk, I could take a bus or call a cab. Surely Rhys would head straight home when he couldn't locate me. The crowd must have scattered in all directions, and he had no way of knowing which way I had been carried. I stayed where I was for a few minutes, looking back just in case he was following, but there was no Rhys. So I set off, walking back in the general direction from which I had come.

It wasn't long before I came to a major intersection and realized where I was: Park Place was the name of the street. Pleased with myself, I waved to the statues outside the National Museum as I walked past it and fearlessly said, "Prynhawn da," "Good afternoon," to passersby. I kept a lookout for cabs, having decided that busses would confuse me. Usually there were quite a few around, but of course now that I needed one the only cabs I saw were whizzing past with passengers inside.

I stopped outside a bookshop to try and decide what to do next. Just as I was about to go in and ask if I could phone Rhys's parents, a horn honked imperiously behind me. I turned, though I knew it couldn't be for me.

It was a black cab, and the driver beckoned to me impatiently, wanting me to come to the window. He was a gray-haired, businesslike man, but I was taking no chances. I walked warily to the edge of the curb and leaned down toward him, staying far enough away to duck back if I needed to.

"You Morfa Owen?" he asked curtly.

Amazed, I said, "Yes, I am . . ."

"Young bloke told me to pick you up and take you to"— he consulted a slip of paper—"Heol y Dderwyn, Number Seven."

Rhys's parents' address. How in the world had Rhys figured out how to find me, when I could have been almost anywhere in Cardiff? Surely he couldn't describe me well enough for a cabbie to pick me out—if one would even agree to try! And why wasn't he in the cab himself? But, somehow, he had managed it. I opened the door and climbed into the back seat.

As I pulled the door shut behind me, the cabbie turned around and stuck a folded newspaper at me. "Here. Said to give this to you, too."

I accepted the paper, bewildered. The cab roared off, and as it dodged through the streets I unfolded the newspaper. It was the *Cardiff Daily*, dated about four weeks ago! Why would Rhys send me a thing like that—and why would it suddenly become important between the time I had been with him at the match, not an hour ago, and now? Not an hour ago . . . suddenly I realized that Rhys couldn't possibly have had time to go home and send a cab out after me. Of course he could have gone straight to the cab company . . . But none of this made sense.

I leaned forward in my seat and said, "Esgusodwch fi . . ."

"Don't speak Welsh," the driver spat.

Taken aback, I switched to English. "Excuse me, sir. I don't quite understand how you knew where to find me."

"Was told to find a short American brunette in front of this bookshop, name of Morfa Owen."

This was absurd. There was no way Rhys could have known I would be in front of the bookshop! Suddenly another thought burst into my mind and I shivered violently.

"Was this young man dark, with short hair, not very tall and built like a rugby player? Was he wearing jeans and a college sweat shirt?"

The cabbie had started to nod his head, but then he paused. "Dark, yes, with a beard. Long hair though, and tall. Never played rugby, too thin. Couldn't tell what he wore under the black coat."

I fell back against the seat, feeling sick. He had followed me even to Cardiff.

How had he found me here? How, how, how?

The cab screeched around a corner onto Heol y Dderwyn and slammed to a halt. Dazed, I opened the door and stepped out, turned to the cabbie and said, "What do I owe—"

"He paid," snapped the cabbie, and sped away down the street.

I stared after him for a moment, then down at the folded newspaper still in my hand. I turned and walked up the path to the Jones' house and knocked hesitantly.

Mrs. Jones answered the door. "Why Morfa, fach!" She

opened the door wider and drew me in. "What happened? Where is Rhys then? You look shattered."

"There was a fight inside the stadium after the match and we got separated . . . I looked around but I couldn't find him so I came home in a cab."

"Now there's a bright girl!" Mrs. Jones smiled and put her arm around my shoulders. "Rhys will be here any time, then. Come have tea. It must have been terrifying for you!"

We walked into the kitchen. I sat at the table, absently sliding the paper onto it. Mrs. Jones glanced at it and said, "Is that today's paper? We have one, you needn't have bought it—"

"No, it's an old one. It was—lying in the cab and I picked it up without thinking."

"Well, never you mind, no one will miss it. Here, drink this."

I sipped the steaming tea slowly, and the slam of a door announced Rhys's arrival.

He came through the kitchen doorway, saw me and was across the room in a quick step. He leaned to hug me quickly. "However did you get here? I was so worried when you disappeared in the crowd!"

"I took a cab . . ."

Rhys smiled and nodded. "Good girl." He pulled up a chair and Mrs. Jones, coming back into the kitchen, poured him some tea and asked him what had happened at the stadium.

"I've never seen a fight there before! But there was a bad brawl, and then a terrible fog came down—"

I stared. "A fog?"

He glanced away from his mother, nodding. "Wasn't it thick? That's why I couldn't see you, even though I knew you had to be close. I thought it was going to rain, it was so dark, but the fog swept in instead. That happens, sometimes. I bet it frightened you, didn't it? Where did you end up?"

"I—I'm not sure. Over by the National Museum," I answered, preoccupied. There had been no fog. I had seen no fog.

There must have been, if *he* had been around. He seemed to bring a fog with him always.

But before, *I* had been the one to see it, while others hadn't.

Rain came in the night. It splattered on the window of Rhiannon's old room as I sat up late, looking through the newspaper. Maybe here, somewhere, lay a clue. It might take all night, but I was going to read every word, from the front page headlines to the advertisements, until I found something that made sense out of all of this.

It was somewhere past the middle of the paper that I came upon the obituary columns. After giving them a cursory glance, I flipped to the next page. Then, before I could read another word, a name I had seen at the top of one of the columns belatedly registered and made my heart jolt painfully. I turned back, and there it was in heavy black print. Ynyr Morgan.

There must be dozens of them in Cardiff, I thought, fighting back, but it was no use.

Ynyr Morgan, 81, formerly of Trevaughan, died today at 12:50 P.M. of heart failure. He had been in the Cardiff General Hospital for several days. Mr. Morgan was a leading citizen of Cardiff and will be missed by all. Services will be held Monday at 1 P.M. Burial is to be in St. Peter's of Carmarthen. Mr. Morgan is survived by his wife, Mrs. Teleri Morgan of Bryn Myrddin, Abergwili, and two daughters, Gwenfair Owen and Angharad Davis of the United States.

And there was a small picture of the delicate-boned, smiling man who could have told me so much, who could have answered all of my desperate questions. Until four weeks ago he had been alive, and we had lived only hours apart. Now my lost grandfather was truly lost forever.

And now if I wanted answers, I knew where I could find my grandmother. There was no question; I would have to find her immediately. But pricklings of fear grew and grew in me.

My mother's nightmare come true. I was going to meet Gran Morgan. And I was going to find out why the idea of this meeting terrified my mother so much that she would break a silence she had held for twenty-five years.

9

My Mother's Secret

"So he *had* moved."

I nodded. The train lurched and I grabbed the arm of my seat for support. "I guess he and Gran were separated, or divorced, or something. It must have been a very long time ago, because the newspaper called him a 'leading citizen of Cardiff.' No wonder I couldn't find him. If I hadn't seen this paper, I never would have."

"I still don't understand that at all." Rhys shook his head in confusion. "Who is this stranger—or what is he?"

"I don't have any ideas about him. I've gotten to the point where I just try not to think about it, because all the thinking in the world isn't going to give me an answer. I've thought all along that he was evil . . . I guess because he always surprised me and seemed as if he was trying to make me do something, so I thought he was threatening me. But now I wonder if he wasn't just trying to give me clues to find Grandfather or Gran. I don't know. I still can't believe Grandfather was so close all that time and I missed him."

The black horse racing down the hill past me . . . the dark man on campus mouthing to me to "hurry" . . . and I hadn't hurried and now Grandfather was dead. His clues hadn't been clear. And the grief Gareth and I had felt on the deserted farmhouse lane four weeks ago . . . four weeks ago . . .

"So are you going to go and see your Gran now? She can't be hard to find, there aren't twenty houses on Bryn Myrddin."

"Yes, of course. I'm pretty sure I know which one it is, anyway."

"You do?"

I nodded. "It's just a hunch, but remember my telling you about a farmhouse lane Gareth and I were on?"

"The one where you felt the sadness so strongly."

"Right. That was about four weeks ago, Rhys, and Gareth asked the time when we got out of the lane and it was almost one o'clock. Grandfather died at twelve fifty. And the name on the mailbox was Morgan."

Rhys was silent for a moment, then said, "I thought you said that house was falling down and deserted?"

I was taken aback. It *had* been falling down and deserted.

"Well, I'm going to go look, anyway, as soon as we get back."

"Today?"

"Wrth gwrs! Rhys, I didn't have any time to lose with my grandfather. I'm not going to let the same thing happen with Gran."

He hesitated, then nodded. "I'll go with you, if you like."

"Thanks," I said, smiling, "but I imagine you'd better see Arianwen! She wouldn't be too happy if you went off someplace with me as soon as we got back from Cardiff, would she?"

"No, she wouldn't," Rhys answered seriously, looking at me so intently that I looked away. "Perhaps you can ask Gareth."

"Gareth!" I looked back at him and laughed. "Oh, Rhys. Gareth is handsome and strong and intelligent and I enjoy his company tremendously. But he isn't in the same class with you or Laney at all, as far as I'm concerned. He uses me, because he's too wrapped up in the Language Society to be interested in dating but it isn't really acceptable for him to appear to not have a girl. And I use him as a Welsh teacher, a political instructor and a sort of handsome escort. It works out well for both of us. But he isn't interested in something like this, Rhys. I would never ask him, and I wouldn't want him with me then anyway. What Gran and I will have to say to each other should be said alone, if she'll even talk to me at all."

"Why wouldn't she talk to you?" Rhys had become very quiet while I was talking about Gareth, and I wondered if he was disappointed in us, for using each other so coolly.

"Why doesn't she communicate with my mother?"

Rhys smiled and shrugged. "Perhaps you can find out."

"I hope so! That's what I'm counting on. I've had enough of this, Rhys. I want to know the answers."

"You've had a caller."

Arianwen sat at our desk, working on a class project, and didn't bother to look up as she coldly answered my "p'nawn da" with the news about a caller. I wonder how she's going to treat Rhys, I thought unhappily, remembering the time, not long ago, when she had been so friendly.

"Ethan again?" I would have news for him this time, anyway.

She pushed the chair away from the desk and turned to look at me with scornful eyes. "I didn't say someone rang you up. A person came to see you."

I felt a stab of old fear.

"A woman," she added carelessly, turning back to her work. "From Trevaughan. Her address is on your bed." I looked there and saw a small scrap of paper. "You're to go see her immediately."

• • •

"This sounds pretty important," said Laney a bit later, as she peeled an orange and dropped the peel into the trash. "Do you have any idea who she is?"

"None at all. From Trevaughan? I don't know any women around here who aren't students, not that I can think of, anyway. And I wanted to go to Bryn Myrddin and talk with Gran Morgan today."

"Hm. Will you be back for supper?"

"Sure, I think so! You'd better come looking for me if I'm not back by then."

"I will, too," Laney said seriously. "Do you want Steff and me to start moving your things up here? It sounds as if Arianwen wasn't the most welcoming thing in the world."

"She wasn't. It makes me kind of sad, but as the Welsh say, 'There we are,' right?"

"Karma," said Laney, nodding and tapping a book with a marker in it on her desk. It was *Shogun*. "Inevitable. You weren't meant to be friends, and so even though you tried to be, you couldn't. Or, as the Welsh put it, 'There we are.'" She grinned at me and we both laughed.

"Yes, if you have time and want to, go ahead and start bringing my things up." I got up and pulled on my long green raincoat. "Here's the address, in case you really do have to come after me. I've memorized it." I put the scrap of paper on Laney's desk by the book. "See you at supper . . . I hope!"

The way through the fields to Trevaughan was familiar from the days Laney and I had gone time and time again to ask about my grandparents. The street name on the paper had even looked familiar and, sure enough, I did find it without any problem. Number Seventeen was a small house, built of whitewashed stone, with a neat little garden that was winter-dead in front. Winter-wild hedges flanked me on both sides as I came up the short walk. At the door,

I stood for a moment, wondering who would answer (The dark man? I wouldn't put it past him to employ a woman the way he employed the cabbie), and what light, if any, she would have to shed on the mystery. Then I rang the bell.

There was no response. I rang again and glanced at my watch. Even if the woman was an avidly religious person, it was rather early for evening services. If this was a trick—

There was a sound of muffled footsteps, then the door rattled and swung open.

A middle-aged, tired-looking red-haired woman stared at me for a moment. Then her hand flew up to her mouth.

"Rydw i'n Morfa Owen," I said. There seemed nothing to add.

Recovering herself, she said very quietly, "Won't you come in, please?"

"Thank you." I followed her into the house and was led to a nicely furnished sitting room. I chose an easy chair and the woman sat across from me. She asked politely if I cared for tea.

"No, thank you," I said and added, "Forgive my impatience, but what I would really like to know is who you are and why you want to see me. And how you knew my name and where to find me."

"I'm so sorry!" cried the woman. "It is you who must forgive me. My head is in such a spin . . . My name is Gillian Lewis. I heard about a young American student at Carmarthen College who was asking about the Morgans in town. The Ynyr Morgans. Years ago, my best mates were Gwenfair and Angharad Morgan."

For a moment the room seemed to swing around me, and I gripped the arms of the chair. This was it. This was the moment I had been waiting for ever since Mam first avoided my questions about her parents.

"I can hardly believe it. It was weeks ago that I was asking around town in Trevaughan!"

"Yes. I'm sorry that it took me so long to come to you. But it was very difficult for me to decide whether or not to do it. It means reviving some old and painful memories. Why, may I ask, do you want to know about the Morgans?"

"Gwenfair Morgan is my mother."

Gillian Lewis gasped and paled. "Your mother! She has married? She is still living? And Angharad—"

"—is married and still living too. I can't understand why in the world none of you kept in touch! What is wrong with you people? Why didn't you write to them, if you were so concerned?"

"I did not know where they were."

"Well, why didn't they tell you? I just don't understand! It all seems really stupid to me."

"That is because you do not know the whole story."

I sighed, and said, "If there's one thing I'm aware of, it's that. But how do *you* know I don't know the whole story?"

"If you knew it, you would not be here. You would not be in Wales. I cannot believe that Gwenfair let you come."

I stared at her. "Why on earth wouldn't she let me come? What is going on here?"

The red-haired woman sat silently for a moment. "It's a long story," she said at last, and rose. "I believe I will make tea, anyway. Tales tell more easily with tea."

I didn't argue with her.

"What do you know about your mother's life in Wales?"

"Very little. I mean, she has always told us a lot about her childhood, but nothing at all about after she left school. She has never even told my father why she left Wales. She still seems to miss it a great deal . . . we kids have never understood why she left at all, or at least why she won't come back to visit."

Gillian Lewis nodded. "Well. The Morgans had a farm not far from here. I lived in this house with my parents at that time. Gwenfair and Angharad and I went to school together and spent almost all of our time out of school at one another's houses. More at theirs than mine, because I was in love since childhood with Madoc Morgan."

"Madoc Morgan? Who is he?"

Gillian looked at me, surprised. "Their brother. She never told you about Madoc?"

"I never even knew she had a brother!"

"Well. I suppose that's not too surprising, if she didn't tell you any of the rest. It's all very tied up with Madoc. He was so handsome. Tall, with a dark beard and such deep blue eyes! Quite a bit older than we were, of course, and I'm quite sure he never knew I existed. But I worshipped him. And his best friend Emrys was very aware of Gwenfair's existence.

"They met at college in Swansea, Madoc and Emrys. The Morgans were Welsh-speaking but very anti-Nationalist, the way some are. Thought the Nationalists were going to be the death of Wales altogether. They were content to be British subjects and didn't want any part of Home Rule for Wales. Well, Emrys was a Nationalist. I don't know how much you know about the political situation here, but you did speak Welsh at the door—"

"I know a good deal about it and have a lot of Nationalist friends at the college."

"Well then. Madoc became fired up with the cause after he met Emrys. He began to attend Nationalist group meetings on the sly. His parents would have been furious if they had known—at least his mother would have. She was by far the worst. If you think there is feeling against Nationalists now, you should have been here then!

"It was all very exciting. Madoc got away with it for a long, long time, which amazed us all because everyone knew that Teleri Morgan was a witch."

"A witch! My grandmother! But that's ridiculous!" It was out before I could remember my conversation on Lammas Street with Rhys about what is a witch; that a witch uses intuition and the mystical powers of the earth and of the elements and can call the Darkness down . . . Some are good and some are bad.

Gillian looked accusingly at me. "You're speaking of something you know nothing about. You are an American. When I say 'a witch,' I don't mean an old hag who rides around on a broomstick and eats children for supper. *That* is 'ridiculous.' But Morfa, there are a few women, and even fewer men, who understand the powers of the earth and know how to tap those powers, to use them for achieving their own ends. I know they have many limitations, and there are as many who use the powers to heal as to harm. But Teleri Morgan was a strange woman. A dark, secretive woman. She had been breathtakingly beautiful in her youth, I was told, and Ynyr Morgan fell in love with the beauty and married it, without taking time to find whether it was solid clear through. It was not. There was something very harsh and self-serving about her. And she used her powers to rule Ynyr and the girls with an iron hand."

"But not Madoc?"

"No, not Madoc. I think she was blind where he was concerned. She loved him obsessively, in a way that she never loved the girls. I used to wonder if he was Ynyr's child at all . . . perhaps she had been married or in love before. No one knew where she came from before she moved here with Ynyr, as his bride. She came from up north, some said, where the powers are even wilder and stronger. Whatever the reason, the powers that alerted her to danger whenever the girls did something of which she disapproved never seemed to work with Madoc. Maybe he had some power of his own that he inherited from her and could put up a shield for himself.

"Madoc and Emrys stayed very close after they left college. Madoc lived in Swansea, and he opened a business with Emrys. We girls would have been brokenhearted at having him gone, but we soon entered college ourselves, and the two boys came back to visit now and again. We three went to Carmarthen College; because we were girls, our parents wouldn't let us go off to Swansea as the boys had.

Then Emrys and Gwenfair fell in love.

"Gwenfair was more beautiful than Angharad, for all they were twins, and far wilder. It's no wonder she and Emrys made a couple, they were very alike. Emrys was wild, too: so fierce about the cause, always out on midnight raids and the like. Exciting, it was. He was handsome, as well, but not my type the way Madoc was. He was shorter than Madoc and very slim, with light brown hair and the pale, haunted look that many of the Nationalists have. It ages them, it does. He had lines around his eyes and he looked quite fragile, but he was wiry in spite of how he looked, and Gwenfair worshipped him as I did Madoc. Of course she became a Nationalist and persuaded Angharad too. I never did any of that. That's when we began to come apart, really. I used to swear to myself that it was all a lot of childish rot and that they'd never accomplish anything by it. And they never did, but it doesn't seem so childish now, somehow. I think I was just a coward, really. It took more daring than I had to take the chances they took. And I loved Madoc, but he didn't love me, and I knew even then he never would, so I probably stayed out of it to spite him, too. It shames me now . . .

"But there we are. The trouble came after the twins got in with the Nationalists. Teleri Morgan found out, as we all knew she would, and forbade Gwenfair and Angharad to go to the meetings or activities of the Society ever again. Then she found out about Emrys and forbade Gwenfair or Madoc to see him. There was such a row, you can't imagine. Gwenfair and Angharad hysterical, Madoc in a rage, renouncing the name of Morgan, Ynyr trying to reason with Teleri, Teleri just as cool as could be in the midst of it all. She told them that this was how it would be and that was that.

"And it was, to everyone's shock. Gwenfair and Angharad and Madoc seemed to calm down and make up with their mother so quickly that it was assumed she had put a spell on them. But I knew better. Madoc could still be going to meetings in Swansea, couldn't he, and there was a spark in the girls' eyes that made me guess they were up to something.

"Then, a week later, Gwenfair went to her parents and told them that she and Emrys had married."

I sat bolt upright, and I could feel the blood drain from my face. "Married!"

"They had been married in Swansea the day before. Gwenfair was triumphant! She knew she had got the better of her mother at last. She told her that she and Emrys were going to live in Swansea, and Angharad with them. It was all arranged. They would leave in two days, when Emrys came from Swansea for them."

Gillian Lewis covered her face and shook her head. "Fools! Teleri could play their game better than they could. She pretended to take the news very well indeed, but no one in town believed it. They knew she was a witch, and I and others tried to warn Gwenfair that her mother would do something yet to stop her. But she was too full of high spirits and confidence to pay attention. 'Jill, don't worry so!' She laughed at me. 'Mam loves me even though she tries not to show it, you know she does, and she wants me happy even if I have to marry a Nationalist! It will be difficult for her, but see, she's trying to adjust already. We have Father's blessing.'

" 'That means nothing,' I told her. Ynyr's opinion had never swayed Teleri before, and I knew it would not now.

"Emrys and Madoc came up from Swansea the next day. Emrys had planned to come alone, but Madoc finished some business and decided to join him at the last minute. His parents didn't know he was in town and he didn't tell them, as they got in late at night. He and Emrys stayed at an inn in Carmarthen, and that's far enough from Bryn Myrddin to keep them from finding out unless they happened to be in town . . ."

"What does Bryn Myrddin have to do with anything?"

Gillian Lewis looked at me in astonishment. "Why, that's where the old farm was! That's where they grew up."

I shook my head violently. "No, Mam always told us that she grew up on a farm near Trevaughan!"

"Well, it is a bit near Trevaughan . . . nearer Abergwili or Carmarthen, though. Maybe she just didn't want to chance your ever finding it."

I was silent, wrestling with a thousand feelings. Gillian sighed deeply and continued.

"Emrys planned to snatch his wife and sister-in-law that night and escape back to Swansea with them before morning. Teleri wasn't expecting them to leave until the next day, you see, so it would catch her unaware. He didn't trust her. But a fog rose that night. It was the worst fog that anyone had ever seen. You couldn't see ten inches in front of your face. It came on suddenly, unnaturally, in the early evening, and there was no way that Gwenfair and Angharad could walk from Bryn Myrddin to Carmarthen without getting lost. They were to meet Emrys on a cliff near Abergwili, a tall, steep hill where he could see them coming from far away. But far enough from Bryn Myrddin to be safe from Teleri. They thought."

Gillian paused and took a sip of tea. Her saucer shook. I thought of the bluffs Gareth and I had passed on our walk to Bryn Myrddin. They were very steep, rising up over the River Towy . . . and suddenly, in a flash of horror, I saw the end of the story.

"Emrys and Madoc had already left for the meeting place when the fog rose. The people at the inn said later that they had been gone over an hour; long enough to be on the cliff waiting. Emrys wasn't familiar with the area; the official version, that the two lost their way in the fog, might have been true if he had been alone. But Madoc had played on those cliffs all his life and could have found his way out of any ordinary fog, or had enough sense to sit quiet until it passed. But that didn't happen. They never returned to the inn, and when Gwenfair and Angharad came the next morning, a search party went out hunting for them. They were found, on the bank of the Towy. They had fallen from the cliff to their deaths."

Gillian rose quickly and walked from the room. I sat like a stone, feeling the pressure of tears, but too stunned to cry. Gillian hadn't said it, but I knew well what she thought was the cause of that fog. Teleri Morgan. The "Gran Morgan" my brothers and I had asked so eagerly about all of our childhoods. The "witch," who had so hated Emrys and had taken so coolly the news of his marriage to her daughter. Not knowing that her son had come back unexpectedly from Swansea with him, she had arranged for him to be lost in the fog and fall from the bluff. How had it happened? Emrys wandering to the cliff's edge, slipping, crying for Madoc's help, Madoc lunging forward to grab his friend's jacket, being pulled off the cliff with him, the long fall that 'I remembered so vividly myself from Llansteffan Castle . . . but theirs had not ended with a safe thump into wet grass. Theirs had ended with a horrendous impact, unconsciousness, the end of their lives.

What hideous justice, that Teleri Morgan, trying to ruin her daughter's life by destroying her son-in-law, had unwittingly destroyed her own son—the only person in the world, evidently, whom she loved.

Gillian's eyes were red and she looked ten years older when she came back into the room. Standing in front of me, clutching a small, flat object, she said quietly, "I haven't spoken of this since Gwenfair and Angharad left. Not to anyone. I haven't relived it for years. It was the most terrible time I have ever known. I destroyed everything I had that reminded me of it or of them . . . letters from the few times we were apart, mementos, and every picture with them in it except for one. I packed it away instead. I cared so much for Madoc, and in the end couldn't bear to destroy the last I would ever see of him."

She sat beside me and turned over a small picture in its frame.

"One of Emrys's friends took it when we were visiting them in Swansea, and I got a copy off him just before the accident. A magic day, that was. That's your mum and Emrys." She pointed to the center figures. The picture had been taken in front of the ruins of a castle. A tall, slim, beautiful girl with bright laughing eyes and long dark curls leaned from where she sat on a little wall to touch the shoulder of a pale young man below her. He too was very slender, with blond hair that reminded me of Gareth's. Emrys smiled at the camera in a way that made my heart turn—he was obviously happy, but with the fragile cheerfulness of one who too often thinks of sad things. Poor Emrys! I looked at the two figures kneeling on the ground.

"Then that must be you and Aunt Angharad. Yes, she does look like Mam there, doesn't she! Not quite as slim, and her hair is shorter . . . her face looks a little wider . . . what were you doing?"

"We had found a wounded sea gull and were trying to help the poor thing—see it there? It's tilted away from the camera and a little behind me . . . it ran away in the end. And there's Madoc, standing over us and thinking what silly twits we are."

I looked at the tall male figure who smiled indulgently at the two girls, and after a second of pure shock my heart leaped painfully. Dark shaggy hair, dark beard, piercing eyes . . . even the ankle-length coat was familiar. I had seen this man on Glannant Road, on the campus, on the bus into town one night . . . but I had only seen expressions of concern, fear, frustration on his face. My dark man was Madoc Morgan.

And he always came in a fog . . .

I looked quickly over at Gillian. Her face was turned away and I could see the trail of a tear on her cheek. I clasped my hands tightly together and said, "What happened when Teleri Morgan found out that Madoc had been killed?"

Gillian wiped her eyes and said, "She had never been a balanced woman. The news of Madoc's death drove her completely insane. She blamed Gwenfair and Angharad for everything, though she never denied plotting Emrys's death. Indeed, she gloated over it. But she screamed for revenge on them for killing her son, and on all Nationalists . . . the village was full of it. Everyone on Bryn Myrddin was a witness at one time or another to her fits. Ynyr left her, which sealed her guilt in everyone's mind. He gave Gwenfair and Angharad money to escape to America and told them to go right away, that there was no telling what their mother would do to them. They left that day, without a word to anyone. The last time I saw Gwenfair was in Carmarthen when they found Emrys's and Madoc's bodies. I will never forget her face . . . but I must not think like that. No one ever heard from them again. Teleri became maniacal when she learned of their escape and tried to murder Ynyr one night at the inn in Carmarthen where he had gone to stay. After that, he committed her to St. Cyril's Asylum. And there she is to this day, if she's still alive. And I'm sure she is. Everyone would know if she had died and be glad, though they would not dare to say so. They would feel that a life that has caused nothing but unhappiness is better ended. Ynyr moved to Cardiff and no one has heard from him either. Poor, poor man . . ."

"He's dead," I said. "I found an obituary in a Cardiff paper. He died four weeks ago. And the notice said he is survived by Teleri Morgan of Bryn Myrddin, Abergwili . . ."

Gillian, who had bowed her head when I told her that Ynyr was dead, shook it now. "No. Either he told no one in Cardiff that she was at St. Cyril's, or they were being . . . kind . . . in deference to Ynyr. He was a good man. A very, very unfortunate and good man."

She turned and looked at me. "And now you, my dear, are in very great danger."

I laughed shortly. "I can't argue with that," I said, and as briefly as I could, I told her about the incidents at Llansteffan Castle and with Arianwen after the Halloween ball. "But I still don't understand why, or where the danger comes from. My friend Rhys speaks of the Powers of Dark and Light, and talks about witches the same way you do. You think all of this is caused by—"

"Your grandmother. I'm sure of it."

"How could it be? If what you say is true, she's been shut up in an asylum for years!"

Gillian clenched a fist. "She's a *witch*, Morfa! Her power doesn't lessen because she's locked away! I'm sure she knows you're here, and that you are Gwenfair's daughter. Perhaps her confused mind thinks that you are Gwenfair herself again. However it is, I will bet that it is she trying to destroy you, she is the source. And time is running out for you, Morfa." She pointed at a calendar hanging on the wall near the doorway. "Tomorrow it will be twenty-two years ago to the day that Madoc and Emrys fell from the cliff to their deaths."

"To the day? Are you sure?"

"I could never forget that date, never, and I'm sure that Teleri will remember it too. The date that Gwenfair 'killed her son.' You must—"

I motioned sharply at her. "Wait. You said twenty-two years ago tomorrow. That can't be right. Mam said it was about twenty-five years ago . . ."

She closed her eyes, calculating, then said, "the way she said her family's farm was 'near Trevaughan?' No, it was twenty-two years ago, I'm certain. Why?"

I was silent for a long time. How much could my world spin in one day? "Because that means that my brother Ethan—he's twenty-one and a half—"

Gillian stared and flushed scarlet. "Gwenfair and Emrys had a son!"

Gwenfair and Emrys had a son, indeed. I remembered the many times I had seen a special gleam of love in Mam's eyes for Ethan, how she leaped to greet him when he had been gone just a few days, how everything he did and said was of the utmost interest to her. I had never felt jealous; it seemed right and natural that there would be a special bond between a mother and her firstborn. But it hadn't been because he was her firstborn, at least that wasn't the main reason. It was because he was the son of the man who had been her first love, whom she had planned to spend the rest of her life with, until her mother had conjured up a fog for him to lose himself in and never return.

I understood now why Mam had struck out at Dad when Sam had overheard their argument. She loved Dad, that was obvious. But her constant concern and fear since I had left for Wales had brought everything back to her so vividly that her self-control had broken at last. When she woke from a frightening dream, perhaps not quite sure if it were real or not, how easy it would have been—in her confusion and despair—to lash out at Dad, though he was only trying to find out what was the matter.

It was certainly clear why she had never referred to our grandmother or kept in touch with her. Grandfather? Well, maybe she *had* kept in touch with him, secretly. That would explain his evidently knowing her married name and Aunt Angharad's, as they had been printed in his obituary. She must never have mentioned him to us because that would lead to questions about her mother.

And that was why she could never return to Wales. Her mother was still here, waiting for her, blaming her for the death of her brother, having the power on her own soil to gain revenge. And she couldn't return because of her own grief over Madoc, whom she too had loved, and over Emrys, her husband, dead under the bluff.

Suddenly an understanding of my mother's pain came over me like a fierce wave, and I covered my face and cried.

"I'm sorry," I told Gillian afterward, but Gillian, smiling, said, "Nonsense!" She patted my shoulder and said, "Now, what to do about you. First, you must stay for supper."

I looked out the window. It was dark already. "Oh, no! I told my—my roommate to come looking for me if I didn't get back by suppertime! I have to leave, and quickly . . ."

"Can't you ring her up? I don't want to think of you walking back alone through those fields in the dark. Stay for supper and I'll drive you back after."

"There is a phone downstairs, if she hasn't left yet and somebody will run up and get her," I said thoughtfully, not relishing the idea of walking back in the dark myself.

I called Laney, reassuring her and filling her in as quickly as I could on what Gillian had told me. Then I ate with Gillian Lewis, telling her about my mother and my aunt and their husbands and children, everything they had been doing since she last saw them twenty-two years ago.

We walked out through the starry night to her car.

"What a beautiful night! You can't see half these stars in the States. At least, not in a midwestern suburb."

Gillian started the motor and I climbed in the other side. We pulled out of the drive backwards, then headed off toward Carmarthen.

"Morfa, I wish I knew what to tell you."

I laughed and said, "You've told me what I've been wanting to know for, well, most of my life! And you've helped me understand the danger I've known I was in. You can't be expected to give me an instant solution!"

"I can hope for it. And if the solution isn't almost instant, it will be too late. Do you have any plans?"

"Yes," I answered firmly. "Tomorrow I'm going to visit St. Cyril's."

Gillian almost ran off the road. "Morfa, no! Don't! I thought I had made it clear to you what a dangerous woman she is, but obviously you still don't understand—"

"I *do* understand. That's why I have to see her! Don't you understand that otherwise I have no way of knowing what her true state of mind is? Or what she plans to do? All you can tell me is how she was twenty-two years ago. Now, from what's already happened, I have to admit it seems as if you're right and she's taking out her anger against Mam on me. But I have to be sure! I have to know what I'm up against! I'll go during broad daylight, and there will be plenty of attendants around for me to yell for if things get out of hand. I have to see her for myself!"

Gillian turned up Glannant Road, and the familiar stone walls rose on either side of the car. "All right, Morfa. I suppose it can't harm you. She doesn't need to see you to do what she wills with you. And perhaps you will get a clue as to what she plans. But be careful—"

"I will."

"And ring me up, is it? Ring me up the day after tomorrow, if you can't do it tomorrow. I'll need to know if you're —all right."

Alive, she means, I thought stonily. "I'll phone. I'll keep in touch. I can't tell you how glad I am that *you* got in touch with *me!*"

She drove through the gates and came to a stop in front of Mair Hostel. Turning in her seat and hugging me suddenly, she said, "I'm glad I did, too. So long as it doesn't do you yet more harm."

I smiled at her, then opened the door and stepped out.

Shutting the door behind me, I leaned back in the open window and said, "One last thing. Can you tell me where Madoc and Emrys are buried?"

"In St. Peter's graveyard. That's down in Carmarthen town—"

"I'm familiar with it. Thank you. For everything."

"I still put flowers on their graves, Morfa."

I smiled. "When I get home, I'll tell Mam that. I'm sure she'll be very grateful."

I waved at the back of the car as it retreated, then glanced up at the light in Laney's room—now mine—and walked into the hostel.

10

Calling the Darkness Down

Every time I went to a class the next day I felt as if I were slipping into a dream world. I guess I said the right things in Welsh, because the severe Mr. Pritchard seemed satisfied with me. But I wasn't aware of what I was doing, and Jim told me on our way out that I looked like I had been up all night. Actually, I hadn't. I had arranged my things in the empty half of Laney's room, our room now, talked to her about Gillian Lewis's story, then gone to bed and slept soundly. Out of relief, I suppose, knowing that the next day the whole business was going to be resolved, in one way or another.

I played my song in Harp quickly and with such fearful, emotionless efficiency that my instructor let me go fifteen minutes early. She could tell that my mind was elsewhere and that it was hopeless to try and coax it back.

By two o'clock I was in the library. I spent a few hours with my pile of old books in the cage. Gradually I put them all away except the ancient one with the power spell in Welsh. Rhys couldn't join me until after his four o'clock lecture to help me finish translating it, so I tried to do it myself but the words were just too difficult. The verbs were all right—I could make out "draw" and "hold" and "chant" and "cast"—but *what* one was supposed to draw and hold and chant and cast remained a mystery. I left the book with my marker in it on the table in the cage, hoping that I could come back with Rhys later. But I was nearly certain that it would be too late. A sense of time running out was bearing down on me with increasing strength.

At four o'clock I could easily envision Dr. Davies's face as he discovered that I was not in class. He knew how much I loved his lectures, but today, instead of being there, I was halfway up Glannant Road toward St. Cyril's. It had been raining and the wet earth was spongy under my feet. Drops of water hung from the tips of leaves all around me. There was a fresh, heavy earth smell in the air, and it was cool though the sun now shone brightly. At home on a day like this, I thought, it would be desperately humid. But here it's lovely. Every day is, even the thin gray misty ones and dark blue stormy ones. How does anyone leave this place?

I let the iron gates clang behind me, walked briskly up the steps and went into the reception hall. If ever I paused, I knew I could never make myself continue. I would turn back and wait shivering and terrified for whatever might befall me at twilight. Instead, I asked to see Mrs. Ynyr Morgan, and in a few minutes was face to face with my grandmother at last.

Teleri Morgan was eighty years old, but the beauty that had entrapped young Ynyr Morgan sixty years ago had not totally faded away. Her eyes and cheeks were sunken deeply into her face, there was a scattering of bristles on her chin, and the arms that clutched the dingy gray robe close up around her neck were gaunt and bony. But her nose was strong, her hair still thick and lustrous, her eyes full of intelligence, purpose—and the glitter of madness.

"Would you excuse us, please?" I asked the attendant who had escorted me up from the receiving room. "We have a great deal to discuss."

"All right, mum, but I'll be just outside if you need me."
The woman left, pulling the door shut behind her.

"Well, Grandmother," I said, controling an insane urge
to laugh.

Light flickered in the old woman's eyes, and her mouth
curled into a tiny smile. For all Gillian Lewis had tried
to prepare me, I was still shocked when the grandmother,
who shouldn't have known I existed said, "Morfa Owen,
come to Wales. You should not have done. There'll be no
going back, you know."

I raised my eyebrows. "You may be right. I like it here
very much. I might decide to stay."

I couldn't control a jump as Teleri laughed suddenly,
a biting, shrill cackle. "Those who are planted, stay! You
will make a nice companion for Ynyr and the Nationalist
at St. Peter's."

"And for Madoc?" I added impulsively.

Her eyes narrowed, and she shrank back in her chair.
"Madoc is not dead. I—I have seen him."

Having sudden doubts about it myself, I changed tactics.
"But if you have seen him, Grandmother, you know that
he has been trying to help me! He tried to warn me away
from you and to help me reach Grandfather before he died.
He knows that what you want to do is wrong. And what
you have done was wrong, too. Why didn't you let my
mother and Emrys alone? What was so horrible about being
a Nationalist?"

"Nationalists!" Teleri spat. "Do they still sing their sad
songs about Wales for the Welsh and about ruling themselves, everyone speaking the "true" language? True
language! I remember a time when no Welsh spoke the
language they believe will save their souls. Their precious
'Welsh.' Ha! It was an invader, too! Who do they think they
are? They are Vikings and Romans, just as the English

they hate are Angles and Saxons and Normans! I was there and I know. We hid in the hills, we daughters of the Moon, and we saw the valleys burning below. They came in long ships, with dragons at their heads and tall masts swaying, and unleashed their swords on our helpless people. And now these 'Nationalists' take the dragon as their symbol! They marched through the valleys, the Legions of Caesar, gold and silver in the sunlight. 'We will civilize you!' they said. 'We will bring the glories of Rome to your barbarous isle.' Glories of their precious Rome. Pah! They brought nothing to the princes and priestesses of the Moon. Like the Dragon-Sailors, they drove us into the high mountains, where we perished slowly. When they could catch us, they burned us. Burned our tools and our bodies until there were none of us left, and then when the Saxons came they fled back to their precious Rome . . ."

"But if they killed all of you," I said, "how can you say *you* rememb—" I fell silent as Teleri fixed a malevolent glare on me. I met her eyes for a moment and what I saw filled me with horror. It was not human, what lay behind those eyes, reminding me of something Rhys had told me about the powers using people, insinuating themselves into the spirits of people who were already weak or inclined to believe their way, and slowly taking them over completely. The body before me was that of Teleri Morgan, but the voice that spoke to me, the eyes that watched my every move, belonged to someone—to something—else.

"Well did we tend our Mother the Earth," she continued. "We worshipped her, we cared for her, until the fruits begged to be picked and the flowers cried out for praise. And her great powers were our powers, all were as one, none suffered. None suffered until the ships and the Legions came, burning and destroying, until the cries of the murdered people were nothing to the weeping of the Mother . . . These 'Nationalist' dogs care nothing for her. They care nothing for me. What do they want to keep alive? The language our tormentors spoke! The legends they became! The buildings they raised to be her chains! They do not want to see what is deep in Wales. They do not want to know of it at all. They whimper and whine, not for the Mother Earth, but for every scar the invaders put on her face, every bruise, every mark of her torment. And so I must retaliate as I can . . . raise a bruise for every bruise on her, a scar for every scar!"

Teleri quivered in rage and her face was white. I was overcome with confusion. I knew that what this power was saying through my grandmother's body was true. The invaders had been terrible to the land of Wales, and to the early, gentle, vegetarian people who had lived there. And most of what the Nationalists were trying to preserve *were* remnants of the invaders, not the invaded: castles, art, literature, language. The Moon-worshippers had left absolutely nothing behind to preserve. If the power that had been in these deeply injured people was still alive, didn't it have every right to be angry, to want revenge?

But the Moon-worshippers could not be brought back. Their lost culture and heritage could not be brought back. Did this power, then, have the right to commit violence against everyone in Wales who was involved in preserving the oldest heritage that they could? Should Emrys have died for loving the only things that kept Wales from being exactly like England? Because those things had been brought here or at least altered greatly by invaders, should they be abandoned in favor of what both Moon-worshippers *and* Nationalists would consider an even worse alternative—the English language, English literature, the whole English heritage? England was an even newer invader.

Looking at the glittering, hate-filled eyes, I realized something else that made all of my momentary near-sympathy trickle away. The Moon-cult, from what little was known about it, had been absolutely pacifist. They were a gentle people who did not under any circumstances cause the deaths or injury of animals, much less people. Though the sympathies and some of the words coming from Teleri Morgan's mouth might be those of the spirit of the Moon-people, the violence was not. Even to save themselves, to achieve their dearest ends, they would not have resorted to the murder of one person, especially an innocent like Emrys. But an evil human would. An evil human, like the human Gillian Lewis had described to me when she described Teleri Morgan.

If an angry, injured power met with an unbalanced, violent human, what would the result be?

It gazed at me with fierce resentment from the chair. Then it laughed, that terrible, shocking laugh, and said, "You have never made the choice, and now is the time."

Choice? *The* choice? I searched my memory frantically, knowing that indecision was a weapon she could use.

"I told him the Power for the Darkness was not in you."

The Darkness! That was it, the Darkness or the Sword. Merlyn told me in my dream that I would have to choose before the time came to use one of them, or it would be too late. But was this the time?

"You are wrong. I *have* chosen." Suddenly I was sure.

"Just as I thought." She looked at my right hand and following her gaze I saw that I had unconsciously clenched it into a fist. Like her, I could almost see the sword I held shining in the afternoon sun that filtered through the window.

"A princely weapon. Unfortunately, one that will not help you."

I stared at the faint phantom sword in my hand. What had the old Welsh book in the library said about making imaginings real? I breathed carefully, gathered my inner strength, made a silent plea to the Dark.

"You are a fool," I told her scornfully. "Gorau arf gwroldeb; the best weapon is courage. And I have the courage to take the Darkness." With that, I lifted the imaginary Arthur-sword of Light and flung it at the window.

The window shattered.

My heart thundered as though it would come through my chest. Teleri was staring at the window, but would turn to stare at me any second, I knew, and she must not know how shocked I was. So I smiled in triumph as the attendant rushed in—and stopped dead, staring at the broken glass aghast, while the thing behind Teleri's eyes regarded me in vicious surprise.

"I will see you at the meeting place," I told it, not knowing what I was saying, and swept past the astonished attendant, out of the door.

Outside the gates, my knees failed and I slid to the ground.

So it was true. However much my heart may have believed it, my head had never before really believed it was possible. There *was* a power, a mental power, that could be pitted against physical things. And I could wield it. I could actually use the inner power.

But the deepest, most cautious part of my mind warned me now. It was foolish to be elated by one small victory. The power I had drawn upon was pitted against a window, an object that had no power of its own with which to fight back. The next time it would not be so easy—and not only because Teleri Morgan had power too. But because in throwing the sword I had shown my hand. She knew now what to expect from me. I had no surprises left for her.

I walked into my room to find Rhys stretched out on my bed, studying. He turned to smile a hello, then jumped up and took me by the shoulders, giving me a shake.

"Morfa Owen, what happened to you?"

I walked over to Laney's mirror and was startled by the reflection. My eyes were brilliant, but with deep, dark circles under them, and my face was flushed.

"Are you sick, fach? We'd better get you to the infirmary, then, is it?"

"No, no, Rhys, thank you, I'm not sick. Where is everyone?"

"In lectures, mostly. It isn't quite five yet."

"I can't believe it! It seems like hours ago since I left."

"Where did you go? Don't you have a lecture now?"

"Yes, but something more important came up." I told him sketchily about my visit the night before with Gillian Lewis and my trip to St. Cyril's to see my grandmother—what was left of her. Rhys turned even paler than he usually was as the story went along and finally sat in the desk chair with a thump. I dropped down onto the bed, suddenly aware that I was exhausted.

"So there we are."

Rhys shook his head slowly. "Morfa, why is this happening? Why to you and your family?"

"Just lucky, I guess. I don't know, Rhys! Of course it probably isn't *just* us. Who knows how many families with bad luck streaks are victims of something like this too? Only they have no opportunity to find out. Like my mother didn't. At least she might have, but she ran away. That's one thing I've learned, Rhys. Whatever this is, I can't run away from it the way she did. No matter what happens, if I survive tonight, I'm going to stay here and study this thing. I'm—why are you smiling?"

"That's good news for us."

I jumped up and hugged him. "Oh Rhys, thank you. That's what I needed to hear about now. Are you going to help me study it?"

Then too late I realized the position I was forcing him into. If he said yes, that meant good-bye to Arianwen, who hated such things and didn't believe in them at all, who had tried so hard to make him disbelieve them too. And it might seem like I was—well, trying too hard to win him to my side. And if he said no—

"Yes. Yes, I'll always help you. Wrth gwrs."

I looked up at him. He looked steadily back at me with those intense, gentle, light blue eyes. And something changed between us, forever.

It did not have to be pursued now. It would be waiting for me. Now it was time to go.

"Well, I have to leave, or I won't be in time for the meeting."

"What meeting? You didn't mention a meeting."

"Tonight is the twenty-second anniversary of the night Teleri Morgan sent my uncle and my—and his friend over the bluff. And it is the first anniversary on which someone has been in Wales for Teleri to destroy in celebration. Whatever is controlling her, or has taken her body over, will rise to a peak of power tonight. If I can strike a blow then, it might damage it enough that it will take it a long time to recover—"

"Morfa, you're going mad! What chance do you think you have? It would be suicide—"

"And what if I don't?" I was almost shouting, not out of

anger with Rhys, but out of fear. "What should I do? Keep being pushed off castle walls and thrown into pools until one of the attempts succeeds? *If* it doesn't come after me wherever I am tonight, which I'm sure it will. I don't think I have much of a chance either, but I have to try! It's better than sitting here and waiting, knowing it's going to come for me, letting it choose the time and place . . . I know I can't destroy it, Rhys, but maybe I can damage it and give myself more time to learn about it, to understand it . . . then maybe I *can* destroy it, in time."

Rhys sat in the desk chair shaking his head hopelessly. "I can't say, 'Stay here and wait for it to get you.' I don't think you can succeed, but I see where you have to try. I'm going to come with you."

"No," I said, shaking my head firmly, squelching the voice inside me crying, "Yes!" "There would be no point. You know nothing more about it than I do, and it would just be confusing. This isn't something you can fight with numbers. I need to go alone. I'm sure of it."

Rhys was silent. "What are you going to do?"

"I'm going to go to the bluffs where they were killed. She'll be there, I know. Then we'll see if I can call the Darkness down. Remember, you're the one who told me that if I didn't have the ability, Merlyn would never have made it one of my options."

"Wish I'd kept my bloody mouth shut."

I laughed, though my head was aching.

"What about the spell in the library? Did you ever get it translated? We could go now—"

I looked at my watch. "No, it's too late, the library closes in ten minutes. Anyway, I need to leave immediately, Rhys. Don't ask me how I know that, but I do. And the spell called for five people, which we don't have. Not with

Arianwen antagonistic and Gareth caring so little about the whole thing. But that's all right, it doesn't matter. I'm going by St. Peter's first, to ask help from all three of them and to try and gather some of the strength that is there. If there was ever a stronghold of *good* Darkness in Carmarthen, that's where it is."

He walked downstairs with me, and I expected a difficult farewell. But instead, he seemed almost preoccupied when we parted and gave me nothing but a distant smile. What bizarre people, I thought, miffed, as I headed for the entrance gates, then dismissed the whole thing. Dusk was falling outside, and shadows danced on the stones in the walls. I passed through the gates onto Glannant Road, walking toward Carmarthen.

Rhys watched Morfa until she was through the gates. Then he dashed toward the Academic Building and the library. On the way, he ran into Laney, coming out of a lecture, books in her arms. They had some quick conversation before he entered the building and she broke into a trot toward Dewi Hostel.

I walked slowly down Glannant Road. Not because I was trying to put the confrontation off, but because it wasn't necessary to hurry. The pattern was set now, and whether I ran or crawled, all would happen as it was going to happen. Karma, Laney had said. That was right, karma. The inevitable. I felt strangely cheerful and whistled as I passed between the rising stone walls. How I loved Wales! A sturdy, white-haired man with a cane asked me directions in Welsh, and I answered in Welsh, which delighted him, as he could tell I was American by my accent. We chatted for a while, and I called, "Da boch chi!" after him as he walked away. How nice encounters like that are, I thought happily as I resumed walking. They could never happen in the States in the same way.

Steff looked up as a knock sounded at his door. He smiled and didn't bother to answer. It was Laney's knock, and she always came in immediately afterward, invited or not. It was part of the texture of their relationship.

She did come in and tossed her books on the bed. He stood, stretched, and kissed her.

"Hiya, Laney fach. What's up?"

Laney sat on the bed and pulled him down beside her. She looked hard into his eyes, trying to read him, to measure him. She had never put him to a test before. She had never meant it to happen at all.

"Steff, baby, we have to have a serious conversation. And it has to be the fastest serious conversation you ever had in your life. Now tell me. Do you believe in magic?"

"Of course," said Steff, surprised, and Laney felt sweat on her forehead from pure relief.

The little town of Carmarthen was quiet, but that wasn't unusual for this time of night. It was closing time for most of the shops, and the pubs wouldn't start jumping until full dark, about an hour away. I balanced on the curb of the tiny sidewalk on Water Street, Heol Dwr, walking heel to toe for my own amusement, reaching out to steady myself against a solid stone wall. This wasn't possible on wide Lammas Street, so there I walked sedately, smiling at the few passersby. Dusk flooded everything and everyone in shades of gray. A young townie walked by with a small sack of chips from the Chinese takeaway, and impulsively

I stopped him and begged a few. He was amused and not bad-looking, but I forgot him instantly as I steered for the Guild Hall, munching my chips. I walked past it. There were no cars at all, and I headed up toward Nott Square.

The librarian was trying to shoo everyone out and couldn't have been more displeased when the dark young student came rushing in at the last moment to ask about books in the cage. Yes, an American student had been in to look at some of the books during the last few days. No, it would not be possible to see them now, the library was just closing. The librarian sighed and quivered as the pale blue eyes pleading with him clouded over with anxiety. It had been a long day, and he wanted to go home to supper. Surely the emergency couldn't be that great. Wouldn't tomorrow morning . . . Well, it was very irregular . . .

I waved to the statue of General Nott in Nott Square, then succumbed to weakness and ducked down Jackson's Lane. The pub was almost empty but the proprietors smiled and welcomed me, knowing me by name. As well they should! I had cornered their cider market. I carried half a pint of it with me to the jukebox and chose two of my favorite songs. Then I sat on a stool at the bar, turning this way and that as I drank and enjoyed the music.

Crying out triumphantly, Rhys scribbled furiously into his notebook. The librarian stood by the cage door, wavering between impatience and a curiosity that he knew would never be satisfied. Finally Rhys finished. Shutting the old book carefully, he handed it to the librarian.

"Thank you, diolch yn fawr, you'll never know how much—" and the rest of the sentence followed him out the library door at a disrespectful run. The librarian shook his head disapprovingly and reached high on a shelf to put the book away.

St. Peter's.

I stood outside the round stone wall, looking at the tiny church inside. The graveyard surrounding the church looked well-filled. I was surprised that Grandfather had been buried here. Well, I thought, maybe it has something to do with Madoc being here. Surely the town was deeply sympathetic toward Ynyr over the loss of his son.

The wall curved up in an arch seven or eight feet tall surrounding an ancient oak door. I pushed on the door, fearful that it would be locked and that I would have to climb the wall, taking the risk of being caught. But it creaked slowly open, and I slipped inside.

Glancing from the address on the slip of paper Laney had given him to the phone book, Rhys felt rising fear. But nodded at last, relieved, and began to dial. The clicking ring of the distant phone echoed in Mair Hostel's tiny booth, and the fear returned as the ringing went on and on. But at last there was a clatter at the other end and the answering voice he had wanted to hear.

"Miss Gillian Lewis? Miss Lewis, this is Rhys Jones. I'm a friend of Morfa Owen. I'd appreciate it if you could come to Carmarthen College at once. No, not yet anyway! Please come, it's most urgent. You can do, then? Do you know where Mair Hostel is? Yes, the one she lives in. Room 10B."

I walked around, looking at gravestones in the gathering gloom. Most of them were very old. Some had moss covering the inscriptions, some were so worn that they couldn't be read at all. There was no one else inside the walled cemetery. The church itself was silent; I guessed that everyone had gone home and that someone came back later to lock the gate.

It didn't take long to find what I wanted. Ynyr's grave was the only one that didn't look aged, and it was in a neat row with the other two, up against a corner of the church. I stood at the foot of the graves, looking at the stones.

YNYR MORGAN, Aged 81.

MADOC YNYR MORGAN, Aged 29.

EMRYS GERAINT WILLIAMS, Aged 28.

Ethan Williams? I wondered if Dad had legally adopted Ethan. Probably. It didn't really matter.

I looked around to see if anyone had come into the yard, but I was still alone. So I leaned down and spoke quietly to the graves.

"Grandad? I'm Morfa Owen, Gwenfair's daughter. I wanted to see you so much, I'm so sorry I missed you. I'm sorry you had such an unhappy life. I hope everything is better for you now. Madoc? Thank you for trying to help me. I'm sorry I didn't pay better attention to what you were trying to say. I'm glad I got to see you, I feel as if I know you a little bit. Even if you did frighten me at first," I admitted. "Emrys? You have a son, Ethan. He's twenty-one now and at college. He's really smart and handsome, you can be proud of him. My mother is married again and she's happy, so you don't have to worry about her. I know she still loves you." I should feel unbearably silly, I thought, but I didn't. Not at all.

I patted the tops of the graves. "I didn't bring any flowers, but I will. Now I'd better go. I have a meeting tonight with Grandmother. Be with me, will you? All of you?"

I turned to go, then jumped as I heard a tiny "chink" behind me. I whirled around, expecting someone to be there, but there was no one. Then I noticed a movement on top of Madoc's gravestone. It was a small stone that must have fallen out of the church wall above. There were a lot of small stone pieces in the walls. For luck, I thought, picking it up and putting it in my pocket. A piece of St. Peter's to carry with me. I walked toward the gate.

Everyone started at the rap on the door. Rhys got up and opened it to reveal a red-haired lady with a drawn face.

"Am I too late?" she cried.

"No, Miss Lewis, it's all right," said Rhys. "Come in." He shut the door behind her.

"I'm Rhys Jones, who rang you up." They shook hands, unsmiling, too filled with fear. Outside it was almost dark.

"This is Laney, Morfa's roommate. She's an American, too. And this is Steffan, another friend." They stood and shook hands with Gillian Lewis.

"Sit down and I'll tell you what is happening."

Gillian perched on the edge of Morfa's bed, pushing her sleeve back to look at a delicate gold watch. "Please hurry," she said anxiously, "oh, please be quick. It's almost half past six, and the danger strikes at seven."

"Seven o'clock? Is that when—"

"That's when the fog rose."

It was as I walked down the North Parade that I first noticed wisps of mist floating by. Actually, they had probably been floating by for quite some time before I noticed. My attention was taken up by the silence of the town. No cars zoomed around the churchyard behind me, to career up Priory Street on their way to the Lampeter Road. It was nearly the time when the pubs would be filling—six thirty-three, my watch said—but there was no one on the sidewalks, there were no snatches of noise and music from opening and closing doors. It was dark, the spacious dark of a clear night, and the street lamps curving down the road ahead of me made me feel as if I were the last person leaving a carnival. I shrugged off a growing unease and crossed the Esplanade.

Standing behind the row of magnificent old houses that marked the southern edge of Carmarthen town, I gazed at my destination. The ground fell sharply in front of me, plummeting to a wide valley below. From my left came the River Towy, making a broad serpentine through the valley. Slightly to my right it veered away and disappeared behind a huge looming mass that sent chills through me—the bluff, towering over the river, clear and ghastly gray, threatening. I must climb down to the valley, set off for the Towy, and then walk the riverbank until I too stood under the forbidding bluff. I dared not think of what might happen then.

Shivering, I hunched down and began my descent. Only a very dim level of my consciousness noticed the thickening gray in the air around me.

It was a small wood, just off campus, but it hid them from all the buildings and lanes. Bending to the ground, Rhys extended his index finger and, touching the grass lightly, walked around in a large circle. Then he touched the grass at the top of the circle and drew an imaginary line with his finger down to the bottom left, then diagonally up and across to the right center, straight over to the left center, to the bottom right and back to the top center. The other three, watching closely, saw he had indicated the figure of a pentacle, a star, inside the circle.

"Now, each of you stand on a point of the star," he said,

moving to the top one himself. Gillian moved silently to his left, Laney to his right, Steff to her right. This left one empty point, which they all looked at, then at Rhys.

"Who is the fifth, Rhys?" asked Laney quietly. "Will it work with only four?"

"No," he answered, and looked at them all, his gaze coming to rest on Gillian. "Who has been involved in this from the very beginning? Who has been Morfa's guide, her friend, though she did not know it at first? Who has been in this far longer than we, with a much greater wrong to avenge?"

"Madoc," breathed Gillian, forcing herself to remain strong.

"He is here," said Rhys, "we will make him here. Whether he comes in true spirit or not, he will be here in our minds."

The others looked from Rhys to the empty point on the star, visualizing Madoc there, hearts pounding.

I reached the bottom of the hill at last and straightened to see where the river ran. To my horror I found that I could only see a few feet in front of me. For the first time, hope and confidence failed me completely. Rhys had been right. What chance did I have? The fog had returned, and chances were, it would take another life, just as it had the time before. The Killing Fog, it would become known as, or the Morgan Curse, once they discovered my identity. There was really no Darkness to protect me, logical though it had seemed earlier. I was alone and not strong enough.

If I dared to walk forward through this fog, even if Teleri were not in it somewhere to greet me, I could walk straight into the river and drown, or sink into the mud-banks at the shore.

Go back, something coaxed me gently. The hill is right behind you. When you reach the top again, the fog will be gone. You can cross the Esplanade and go back into Carmarthen to your friends. You can all spend a nice, warm evening at the Ceff, drinking cider and laughing and being glad you're alive. There is no reason for you to put yourself in this peril. It will not bring Madoc or Emrys back. Your mother is safe and well in the States. She will never return to Wales. Nothing will be changed. Why go on? Go back. Don't be a fool. Don't be a fool.

I found myself halfway back up the hill with no memory of the climb.

But I stopped, trying in vain to peer through the thick, milky fog. Sure, it would be great to go back—great for tonight. Provided a car didn't flatten me on my way up Glannant Road, or a stone wall collapse as I walked by. But what about tomorrow morning, and all the days ahead? I would never be able to live without the fear that death was around the next corner. Even if I escaped, the threat could pass on to my children just as easily as it had passed on from my mother to me. The Darkness had worked for me once, and while that was no guarantee that it would choose to do so again, at least I knew it did exist. Who was I to lose faith in it now? And if I did, what would be left for me to believe in? I was committed. There was no turning back.

I shuddered. The fog, wet and cold, clung to me, dampening my coat. I hesitated a last time, then picked my way back down the hill and plunged forward in the direction where I had last seen the river flowing under the bluff.

Laney watched Rhys walk slowly to the center of the circle. She heard him speak words of greeting to the Powers of the North, South, East and West. She welcomed the Darkness and the Light with him and, with the others, concentrated, trying her hardest to believe in what they were doing. It was no part of her life. She was an American in Wales for a year, going home at the end of that year with wonderful memories of Wales, but no less an American. This was foreign and sinister to her, but she knew that what was happening to Morfa was real. She also knew that Morfa belonged to Wales with a fierce, sad belonging that she herself would never experience at all, anywhere. She did not want to experience it. It was too much, too much of a commitment. Clutching Steff's hand, she angrily, fiercely willed Wales to accept Morfa.

Steff felt the squeeze and understood, as much as he was able. He had been brought up by parents who believed in the Old Knowledge, so although this was very sudden and he had never been involved in anything like it before, it did not frighten him and he, too, believed in it. He knew what an effort trying to believe was for Laney and was proud of her effort. There were those in the group who were closer to Morfa, but he cared very much for her and hoped with all his simple, sincere heart that this ritual would work. He had absolute confidence in Rhys. Glancing over at Gillian Lewis and seeing the strained look on her face, he smiled a small, reassuring smile.

Gillian felt as if she were caught up in a very old nightmare. She had denied the power when she was young, but not since it had destroyed Madoc and Emrys, had broken Gwenfair's life, not now that it threatened Gwenfair's daughter. All these long years she had tortured herself with the thought that she might have been able to help them in some way. It had festered inside her until she had retreated from the world and seldom left Trevaughan. She had agonized over whether to talk with Morfa or not, wavering violently until she could no longer stand it. Now Morfa was facing the power because of her, because of Gillian Lewis . . . and if it destroyed Morfa too, how could she ever live with herself? She glanced bleakly at the empty point on the star, wondering if Madoc were really there, if he was still in some strange way alive and caring about what happened to Morfa. Oh, Madoc, she said to him silently. Please be here. Help Morfa. But please, please, don't let me see you. It would kill me, Madoc, I couldn't bear the pain of losing you again.

Rhys returned to his place. He took Laney's and Gillian's hands. Laney took Steff's, and Steff and Gillian reached for the phantom hands of Madoc. Gillian closed her eyes, sweat running down her face despite the cold, clinging fog. Oh God, she thought miserably. Is that really a pressure against my hand, or am I imagining it? I dare not look. I dare not.

From many feet away, Arianwen watched. She was hidden behind some bushes and certain that they had not seen her. What were they doing? Obviously a rite of some kind. She saw Rhys move to the center of the circle and turn ceremoniously to each of the others. What was he saying? Where was Morfa? And Gareth? She felt angry, betrayed, but she knew now she could not break them up, ruin their ritual as she had planned. Morfa's coming had been a curse for her, the girl who had looked so much like her. Morfa had taken Rhys away from her forever. Arianwen knew that Rhys and Morfa lived in a different Wales from the one she knew. It was a Wales through which blew the winds of fourteen hundred years past. *Did* it exist, somehow, alongside the one she knew and loved, the modern Wales? She realized that if it did, she did not want to know.

Rhys returned to his original place and they all seemed to be linking hands, though two just held their hands out in the air. No, there was someone holding them. How had she missed him before? Gareth? No, he was taller and dark. Unfamiliar . . . a bloke from town, no doubt. Anyway, it looked as if the real business was about to start. Time to leave, Arianwen said to herself, turning away at last and heading back to the hostel with tears in her eyes. Time to leave, before something happens that makes me believe.

Gareth threw the dart with such skill that the win looked simple. The small audience that had drawn around the players in the Ceff cheered, though it could hardly be heard over the general pandemonium. Gareth bowed, smiling his most reserved smile, inwardly very pleased. Moving to the bar for a drink, he noticed Cemlyn, this year's president of the Language Society, coming in the door.

"Shw mae, Cem, old bugger!"

"Shw mae, Gareth." Cemlyn twisted out of his jacket and let it fall behind the piano. "Guinness," he said to the bartender, then turned to Gareth and said, "Been out lately, mun?"

"Na. Why?"

"There's a fog risin' thicker than an omelette. Old Dai Jones says it's the worst he's seen since the one twenty-two years ago that got the bloke from Abergwili. You could swim through the stuff."

"History repeating itself, is it?" Gareth grinned, then poked his friend in the side and motioned toward a girl sitting in a corner with friends. She was blonde and very pretty. "Wouldn't mind getting caught out in it with that one, is it?"

"Aye," Cemlyn agreed, and both laughed. The bartender

set their drinks in front of them, and they picked them up at once, still chuckling.

"Here's to her kind," said Cemlyn. They clicked glasses and said, "Iechyd da!"

The dark mass that suddenly loomed high in front of me nearly gave me heart failure before I realized that this must be the bluff. I took a step forward, and then I was staring straight into the sunken face of Teleri Morgan.

Heart leaping, I choked down a scream and stepped back. "You!"

Teleri smiled. Her eyes were black, with no spark of human feeling. "And you. I am surprised. I thought you would have turned back long ago."

I drew a breath. "Well, as you can see, I did no such thing. If it wasn't now, it would come eventually."

"Yes," and she advanced slowly toward me. "It would come eventually."

Behind me I heard the rushing waters of the Towy.

It began as a soft humming. Laney expected to feel self-conscious, but found that she did not. All four had their eyes closed, breathed slowly and evenly, seeing power course up from the heart of the earth into their bodies, to rise in tall pillars above them. "Pretend you are the power," Rhys had told them earlier. "Send your body deep down into the earth to tap power from it. It has plenty to spare and will sustain you. Then send the power shooting up through your body and try to touch the stars with it. See in your mind's eye these pillars of power, swaying above you, to meet with the Darkness high in the heavens." And Laney was trying with all her heart.

The humming rose and fell, grew louder, then softer, but ever stronger. Slowly Steffan, Gillian and Laney began to feel themselves pulled into the circle, becoming the star, losing their selfness. Rhys chanted softly: "We are the Powers of the Earth. We are the Powers of Fire. We are the Powers of Water. We are the Powers of the Air. We are the Powers of Light. And we are the Powers of Darkness!"

Eyes tightly closed, all could see the five pillars soaring above them, and then the pillars wavered, fell to one side, tops wrapping around one another to form a cone. A tall cone of power, to entrap and funnel the Darkness.

Rhys said, "We are between the Worlds."

I took another step backward and stopped quickly, feeling my foot sink into the mud of the riverbank. Teleri's mad face, pale and close, sneered into my own. "You dared to challenge me! You are nothing but a child."

Gathering my wits together, I said, "And you are nothing but an old withered hag."

The empty face looked shocked and formed a hideous smile. "I am your grandmother, Morfa fach. Your loving grandmother, who wants only to hold you close. Come, dear, let me hold you . . ."

I risked another half-step back. "You are not my grandmother! My grandmother died twenty-two years ago. You are an old crab that crawled into an empty shell."

"You think she did not know what she was doing when she raised the fog?"

I pulled my coat tightly around me and gulped down my fear. "If she did, then she was never my grandmother."

The humming was faster, wilder, and the cone swung from side to side. All four began to feel electricity, or something like electricity, running through their bodies. It seemed to be coming out of the ground, or was it out of the sky? Steffan tried to move his foot and found he could not. It didn't matter.

"You know what is going to happen, don't you?"

I closed my eyes, then opened them quickly. "You are going to try to kill me the way you killed Madoc and Emrys. But that isn't going to happen."

"You are wrong. They will find you on the riverbank tomorrow, or in the river, floating face down, after the worst fog in twenty-two years. And won't it interest them when they find that you are niece to one who was killed then! Interesting, but no more. There is no other connection. And everyone will tut-tut about a stupid American girl who didn't know enough to stay away from the river in a bad fog. Maybe if you're fortunate, they'll bury you in St. Peter's. You can molder with your grandfather and the dog Nationalist and—and—"

"Madoc!" I shouted, hoping desperately to distract her. But my heart froze as I saw that the name no longer affected her. The last whisper of Teleri Morgan's spirit had gone.

"Yes, the unfortunate Madoc. I believe there is room for you next to his grave."

Madoc's grave.

Teleri came at me suddenly, reaching out. And staring into her eyes I saw not a woman but a ghastly white, seething terror, gurgling and laughing and spinning toward me from a different reality, clutching at me with my grandmother's skeleton hands.

I grabbed at my pocket frantically.

The humming rose to a crescendo and the cone drew far, far back.

I pulled out the little stone from St. Peter's and stepped back . . . using the last of my strength of will to give it the Power of Darkness . . . and then feeling myself slip and begin to slide down the muddy, treacherous bank.

With all their mental force, they pulled the Darkness down into the cone and hurled it toward the Towy.

I hurled the stone.
It flew past Teleri Morgan, who ducked and staggered.
It hit the bluff with a tiny thump.
There was a tremendous roar. I heard Teleri scream— a wailing, inhuman shriek—as I looked up and saw darkness crashing in, covering me, and then I could neither see nor breathe, and everything was darkness.

Epilogue

"Miss Owen?"

The campus infirmary nurse stuck her head timidly around the door. I smiled at her inquiringly.

"The police are here. Could you talk with them for a moment then?"

I nodded. She disappeared, and the door swung open wide to admit two uniformed officers. They stood just inside, seeming ill at ease.

I indicated two chairs near the bed and said, "Please sit down." They took off their caps and said, "Thank you, Miss Owen."

The one nearest me said, "We found your grandmother's body, Miss Owen. It was very deeply buried in the avalanche. I'm sorry."

I felt a strange twinge of grief. Then it was gone.

"Miss Owen, could you please tell us what happened last night? How did you come to be walking by the river with your grandmother?"

I had been thinking about this moment and what I would say. There would be no use telling the whole truth unless I wanted to take my grandmother's place at St. Cyril's.

"I had visited the graves of my grandfather and uncle at St. Peter's. I went down the hill to the river afterward, wanting to walk and think a little. This was before the fog rose. Then I met my grandmother who had somehow escaped from St. Cyril's. The fog trapped us. And then the avalanche came when we were waiting for the fog to lift, so we could find our way home."

"Was there anything at all that you did that might have triggered the avalanche?"

I hesitated. "I threw a stone against the bluff."

"Ah. How big was this stone?"

I held my fingers about two inches apart. "About this big and round."

The officers exchanged amused glances. "I doubt, Miss Owen, that a stone that size could bring down half of Pen Morfa!"

I caught my breath. "What did you say?"

"Pen Morfa. It's Welsh, the name of the cliff that fell. 'Pen' means head, and the morfa is the stretch of land where the river meets solid ground. Morfa was also an early Welsh goddess."

"Now," said the other officer, bored, "I think that will be all, if we can just get some vital statistics." He took out a pen and clipboard. "First name?"

"Morfa," I said.

I sat on the bench across from the Ceff in the afternoon sun, waiting. Since the incident at the Towy, I had felt oddly alone, unreachable and unable to reach anyone else, though of course that was nonsense. But there was no one now to understand what I had felt, except maybe Rhys. Rhys, who had also touched the Darkness, called it down into his hands.

"You should have seen him, Morfa! Except then of course there would have been no reason for us to have been there." Laney had laughed as she told me this, sitting by my hospital bed. But even laughter and jokes couldn't hide her real awe for what had happened. "He was so powerful. You could tell that he was meant to do just what he was doing then, and nothing else. You and he, Morfa, you aren't really of this world, are you? I wonder how many of you are out there all over the earth, some knowing and more not knowing who they are and what they can do. Is there some great purpose to it all, do you think, or do you all have your own individual quests?"

"I don't know," I answered honestly but unsatisfactorily. "I feel 'of this world,' though."

"Oh, I don't mean like aliens, of course, or 'wrth gwrs,' as you so crudely put it. Didn't think I knew the crummy language, did you? Well, I might be a bit quicker than you think!" She airily waved off my protests and continued. "I meant that you are from an older earth. What is real for you just doesn't exist for most people. I thought it never would for me, but I guess what I saw last night shocked some sense into me. I still don't want to be involved, mind you! I'd rather die. After all, what if you found out that you had this tremendous power and had an experience like you or Rhys had, and then it never came to you again? I don't think I could stand that. I'd rather never experience it at all."

And she was right, of course. What if the power deserted me, now that it had achieved Teleri's destruction? What if I had been used for that purpose, and now that it was over with, the power had poured out of me forever? Could I live with that?

I wasn't naive enough to think that whatever it was that had threatened me had been destroyed with Teleri Morgan's body. Thwarted temporarily, yes. But it would always come back in different ways, over and over again, until someone found a way to destroy it, found out what it really was.

And I wanted to be that one. I was determined to be. What else could I do now? Settle down somewhere quietly in the States, be content to live an average life, knowing all the while that it was out there somewhere building up strength, getting ready to strike again? And even if I knew somehow that it would never gather that strength in my lifetime or my children's or even their children's, I was trapped anyway. I had touched the Darkness, had known the feeling of channeling a cosmic power with my own hands. I could never forget that feeling. Wasn't it a gift, after all? If it was true, as Rhys had told me, that Merlyn wouldn't have offered it to me if I couldn't use it, wasn't it also true that since I *could* use it, since I *had* used it, it was my right and duty to keep on doing so?

But all of this meant nothing, really. If the power didn't return, there was nothing I could do about it. Who declared my "rights"? Who assigned my "duties"?

Restless and unhappy, I rose and walked up Heol Dwr. A sudden shower of rain began to come down in broad sunlight, as it so often did here. Shoppers retreated into doorways, forming little knots of patient people who chatted cheerfully, knowing that these showers never lasted long. I stood in the rain, looking at their faces. And then I knew what would happen if the power never returned. I would be desolate for a while, but then, slowly and relentlessly, everyday life would take over again. The life force was too strong. If I needed to forget all of this in order to go on living without it, then I would forget. Never completely, but the mystery and magic of what had happened would fade until it came to rest at the back of my mind, hovering between reality and fantasy.

The rain stopped, and those who had taken cover set off about their business. I hesitated, unsure of where to go, then felt gentle hands on my shoulders.

"How about a drink, then, is it, boyce?"

I turned, laughing, meeting Rhys's sparkling eyes, and said, "Wrth gwrs!"

We clasped hands and headed back down Heol Dwr toward the Ceff.